# Tell Me a Lie

## Madigan River Book 1

# Jannie Lund

Published by Jannie Lund, www.jannielund.com

Edited by Heather at A Plot Whole, www.aplotwhole.com

Cover art by Jannie Lund

ISBN 978-87-999401-0-3

A massive thank you to Stacie for the encouragement and hand-holding, to Heather for the red pen wielding and much appreciated no-nonsense attitude, and to all the people in my life who made me stronger while writing this book.

Jannie Lund

# Chapter One

The weather was perfect for a funeral.

Skye pulled her jacket closer and wished she'd thought to bring an umbrella. Pastor Simmons droned on and on in that wit-numbing way of his, seeming not to notice the rain or the chilled crowd around the grave. Skye looked around again, trying to be subtle about it. Even to herself, she was reluctant to admit who her eyes were searching for. When she had to admit it anyway, she explained her actions away as natural curiosity. After all, if Thomas Madigan's unexpected death didn't bring his scattered sons back together, nothing probably could.

Hunter was there, of course, head bowed in respect next to the oak casket. He was the one who had never left, never wanted to. Steady as a rock he was, and twice as reliable. Down-to-earth Hunter Madigan was always ready with a smile and a helping hand, even when he had more than enough on his own plate. Skye was glad to count him among her friends.

Julian was there, too, and he wasn't fooling anyone with the dark sunglasses. They weren't to hide his grief or tears. Skye knew he wore them in an attempt to dull yet another hangover. He always did. Julian had been an angry child, an even angrier teenager, and now he was an angry young man. Whether his father's death would fuel or soften his anger was impossible to say. Because she had a soft spot for him, Skye hoped he'd be able to find some peace within himself soon. It had to be exhausting to be so miserable all the time.

Letting her eyes roam over the crowd of people who'd defied the weather and turned up to say a final goodbye to the great-great-grandchild of the town's founding father, Skye spotted the third Madigan brother.

Reid had been gone for long periods of time in the past decade, only ever returning when he needed to make a buck for his next sailing adventure. It had been at least three years since he'd been home last. His sun-bleached hair was in a ponytail, and the earring glinting in his ear gave him the look of a pirate. She imagined he'd be pleased to give off that vibe.

That left Cameron, the one Skye had been looking for all along. As far as she knew, he hadn't actually been back in Maeville in the past six years. The talk of the town was that he was too busy with his music career in Nashville. Cam had always wanted to be a star—a country music star, first conquering Nashville and then the world. "Everyone will be singing along to Cameron Madigan someday," he'd often told her when they'd been young, naïve, and stupidly in love. Skye had dreamed of penning the songs Cameron would make his mark on the music business with, but only one of them had ever really gotten a taste of their dreams.

The pain of a shattered heart had long ago faded into a violent sting now and again when she allowed herself to think about the past, but it had been a serious wound when Cameron blasted out of town alone chasing the dreams they had once shared. The dozen or so postcards she'd gotten in the first year had done nothing to soften the blow, but time had been a great healer.

So had her common sense.

It really wasn't for her own sake that she was keeping an eye out for Cameron. It was mostly for the Madigans. The last thing they needed was the town gossiping about Cameron's absence. And okay, it was for her own sake, too. Pride had kept her from reaching out to him, and she figured this was her chance to see if she'd healed as well as she hoped she had. Six years was a long time, but Cameron Madigan wasn't just anyone. He'd been a star long before he'd left town, at least in a young Skye Jones' eyes.

The rain grew heavier and almost drowned out the mourners singing the last psalm. Skye didn't sing along, afraid her teeth would start clattering if she opened her mouth. She was tempted to leave, but since her daddy had been kept from attending by one of the Henderson kids needing a cast on his newly broken leg, she knew he'd demand a full replay when she got back to the clinic. So she stayed, wondering if she'd ever get warm and dry again.

The casket was being lowered into the ground when Skye finally spotted Cameron approaching—and felt her heart beat for the first time since he'd left. Damn him. The black Stetson angled to keep the rain out of his face and the heavy jacket didn't conceal his identity for a second. Hands buried in his pockets, he sauntered—Cameron Madigan still didn't just *walk* anywhere—closer. He stopped, standing alone a small distance away as his father's casket disappeared from view. The past six years melted away, and despite whatever reasons Cameron had for staying away for so long, she knew plain as day that he was hurting.

That, in turn, hurt her. Whatever healing she thought she had done had clearly been a figment of her imagination. Part of her wanted to go to him, offer her support. It seemed like she had always wanted go to him. After he'd left, it had become necessary to learn not to, but old habits died hard apparently. Especially now that he was so close.

For better or worse, Cameron Madigan was back—in town and in Skye's life. And she needed to deal with it somehow.

\* \* \* \*

It wasn't that he had doubted the text message Hunter had sent, but seeing his brother helping to lower a casket into the ground drove it home. Their daddy was gone. Cameron swallowed with some difficulty and was grateful for the bad weather that gave him the perfect excuse to keep his head down.

Soon after he had arrived, the nameless, faceless people around the grave began to scatter. Instead of revealing himself, he wandered deeper into the cemetery, figuring everyone would be in a rush to get out of the rain, allowing him to say his goodbye in private. It wasn't going to be an easy one.

He hadn't meant to be late, but his car had broken down halfway between Nashville and the drowsy North Carolina town he'd once called home, and fixing it had taken a while. Now he supposed that hadn't been such a bad thing. A lot of people had turned up to say goodbye to Thomas Madigan, and Cameron wasn't in the mood to deal with any of them. Of course, he should have expected that people were on the lookout for him, and he hadn't gone far when someone cleared their throat behind him. Resisting the urge to sigh, he turned around.

"You made it." Looking proper in a in a suit and grief swimming in his eyes, Hunter looked as much the perfect son as he always had. The old resentment bubbled up instantly, as though years hadn't passed since the brothers last saw each other.

The words were stuck in Cameron's throat, and instead of spewing his anger he just nodded. If the words ever got unstuck, they were bound to come out sounding nasty. It was more than the years of separation that stood as a wall between him and Hunter.

"I'm glad." Hunter's neutral tone left Cameron unable to tell if he was being sarcastic or not.

The rain began to slow, not that it mattered since they were both already drenched. And had nothing to say to each other. Good to know nothing around there had changed, apparently.

"Are you coming back to the house?" Hunter asked.

Cameron nodded again.

Shifting his weight from one foot to the other, Hunter looked away. "Well … I'll see you there."

Watching him leave, Cameron stuck his hands into his pockets. He and Hunter had been close as kids, but when they had gotten too old to kick a ball around and wreck havoc with their slingshots, they had stopped having anything in common. He had resented Hunter's love for their dad, the sawmill, and the town. The need to go, to do, to accomplish that had raged through Cameron's body had never been present in Hunter's, and it had been easier to sneer at his younger brother's complacency than attempt to understand it. That hadn't changed either.

Alone in the cemetery, Cameron wandered back toward his father's grave.

It was ridiculous that larger than life Thomas Madigan was nothing more than bones in a box now. For all the disagreements, arguments, and fights over the years, not to mention the fact that they hadn't talked to each other in six years, Cameron always thought they would some day figure things out. Now, with the rain and the tears mingling on his cheeks, Cameron realized that would never happen. He had missed his chance. But it was more than sadness and grief that filled him. Resentment simmered near the surface. It wasn't like the stupid, old bastard had ever asked him to stay, was it? He'd never made amends for his harsh words or for his lack of attention. Cameron had never apologized either, but he had sure as hell had tried to get the old man's attention. His respect. Hell, his love. It didn't necessarily make someone a bad person that they weren't a chip off the old block.

Reaching the open grave, the anger and the resentment evaporated at the devastating sight of the casket, and so did the words he had planned to say. So he stood in silence for a few minutes, then tipped his hat and turned his back on the old man for the last time

Driving through the well-known streets of Maeville brought up a lot of memories. It still looked pretty much like it had six years ago, but Cameron knew that, like him, things were bound to be different beneath the surface. Old, familiar faces would be gone, replaced by new, unfamiliar ones. Changes in the people he knew brought on by age and experience, places and hangouts dear to him destroyed. Nothing would probably be the same once he got a closer look. The old resentment at small town life was not as strong as it had once been, because since he'd last seen the familiar streets of the town he'd grown up in, he'd gotten a valuable lesson in what home meant.

The big house on Madigan Avenue would be full of changes, too, even if it looked exactly like it did the day Cameron had left town. For one, it wasn't Thomas Madigan's house anymore. It would no doubt be Hunter's, although heaven only knew if inheriting it would be enough to drive him away from his cabin up river where he guarded his privacy with the ferociousness of a rabid dog. Okay, nothing about Hunter was actually ferocious. He was too laid back for that, but he did value his personal space above almost all. Or had. Cameron knew next to nothing about what more than half a decade had done to his brother.

Cars lined both sides of the street and were crammed into the wide driveway. He didn't particularly feel like going into the house and dealing with the army of curious neighbors and distant relations that he barely knew. His daddy hadn't had any friends; he was always too busy making his mark on the world for such frivolous things. In that aspect, Cameron knew he was a lot more like his daddy than he wanted to be. Just like he knew that despite the reservations he had about it, his duty was to go inside. He couldn't hide like he had done at the cemetery.

He had to park around the corner. As he approached the white three-story plantation style house that had housed six generations of Madigans, a wave of nostalgia hit him right in the chest. It was the only real home he had ever known, and if he had missed anything or anyone in Maeville, it was that. Having a home and belonging somewhere—not that he would ever admit that to anyone.

There was a guy on the front porch braving the rainy bursts of wind, sitting on the ground with his back against the house and puffing enthusiastically on a cigarette. The hood of the black sweatshirt hid most of his face, and a beer can sat under the nearby rocking chair. The front porch on the Madigan house sure hadn't been used for sipping sweet tea in a long time. It seemed fitting to have some drunk sprawled there. Cameron walked past him, steeling himself before he pushed the front door open.

The murmur of voices met his ears at the same time as the smell of food reached his nose. Groups of people were standing in the large entryway, and everyone stopped talking and turned to look at him. The silence quickly spread through the whole house, except for the odd harsh whisper of what he was sure was his name. It wasn't so different from standing on a brightly lit stage in front of an unhappy audience.

Determined not to let his nerves show, Cameron slowly took off his soaked jacket and hung it on the hallstand. He wanted to keep his hat on, but hung that too. His hands were less than steady as he ran them through his hair, securing it with an elastic band, and he quickly shoved them back into his pockets when he was done. He tried a polite smile for the nearest group of people, and he wondered if it looked as forced as the ones they sent back at him. Maybe it wasn't too late to grab his hat and make a quick exit.

\* \* \* \*

"Cam!"

At Reid's exclamation, Skye's head turned automatically. She had been perusing the large collection of framed photos on the antique bureau, surprised to see Mr. Madigan had included several of herself and Cameron. They had been the talk of the town right before Cameron left them all in the dust in pursuit of Nashville's bright lights. "When's the Madigan boy gonna pop the question to the doc's pretty, young Skye?" had been the most asked question after Sunday church.

People thought she hadn't known, hadn't heard. But she had, and she had wondered, too—until she had found the answer quite clearly in a pair of disappearing taillights on Cameron's car as he left her and Maeville behind.

Skye saw the unmasked surprise on his face when Reid strode over and wrapped him in a hug. It took a moment before he returned it, and afraid he would look over at her getting teary about the brotherly reunion, she turned away and slipped out of the room. Seeing him again was sending so many of her feelings spiraling out of control, and she wasn't even sure if she'd preferred not seeing him at all.

"Bless his heart, but that Cameron Madigan never did have any sense of timing, did he?"

Skye smiled politely at the Madigan's neighbor, Mrs. Harris, who was famous for having at least one opinion on every subject. "At least he's here."

"As he should be." Mrs. Harris peered around Skye through the door. "Is that what them music stars look like nowadays?"

Skye swallowed a sigh. "I think it's what grieving sons look like. Excuse me, Mrs. Harris. I think Camille needs my help."

The last thing Camille needed was help, but Skye wasn't above using her best friend as an excuse to get away from Mrs. Harris. The woman could gossip both your ears off if you gave her the chance, and Skye wasn't in the mood to hear what Mrs. Harris and the other gossipers in town thought of Cameron returning. She'd hear that soon enough.

Skye found Camille in the kitchen, where she was wrapping up casseroles and arranging cakes on plates. South of the Mason-Dixon, nothing eased grief like a good casserole.

"Save me."

Camille looked up. "From what? Cam? I've had at least seven people come out in the last five minutes to tell me he's back. You okay?"

"From Mrs. Harris actually." Skye grabbed a cookie and sat down at the breakfast bar. "And I'm fine…I think."

Camille kept busy. It was her default mode to take care of people, help out, manage, and put everyone else's needs above her own. No one had asked her to be on kitchen duty at her boss' funeral, but she did it anyway. Did things like that so often that Skye bet Hunter hadn't even thought twice about letting Camille handle everything.

"Have you talked to him yet?" Camille asked. She was the only one who knew exactly how many bitter tears Skye had cried over Cameron.

"No. I'm not even sure I want to." She nibbled on the cookie without tasting it. "Where's Hunter? I haven't seen him since I got here."

"He's around." Camille gestured vaguely. "I'm not sure he's realized that he's the host today. And don't get me started on Julian. Last I saw him, he was smoking and getting buzzed on the front porch."

"I know they're all adults, but today they're just lost boys, aren't they?"

Camille hummed in agreement as the kitchen door opened. Hunter wrestled off his tie and sighed as he crossed the room to sit down next to Skye. "One minute. I just need one minute's peace and quiet."

"Take as many as you want. I'll guard the door." Skye pushed the plate of cookies his way and squeezed his arm.

The Madigans had always played a central role in her life, from her disastrous past with Cameron to a treasured friendship with Hunter, and she hated to see any of them hurting, especially Hunter. He was the one who had found their father dead, who had tracked down Reid and Cameron, and arranged the funeral. With Camille's help, he had also kept the family's sawmill running.

"I don't reckon it's very polite to boot people out the door," he lamented as he devoured a cookie.

"Probably not," Skye agreed.

"Well, darn." He turned his head and looked at her. "Cam's here."

She nodded. "I know. In the immortal words of Mrs. Harris, 'As he should be.'"

"You okay?"

"Perfectly fine. Though, even if I wasn't, it's not important on a day like today."

Hunter shrugged. "I don't know about that. Sure, he left and made something of himself, but there's strength in staying, too, making it work with what you've got. Like you did. Like I did. And now he just rolls back into town, late for his own daddy's funeral, and thinks he's all that. Reid breezes into town much the same way, although what he's got to show for himself except for a tan, I've no idea. And Straw...fucking kid is drunk on the front porch, showed up at the service with a hangover, but they're the ones getting noticed. Cam's here. Reid's here. Oh, look, Straw made it to his daddy's funeral. Shit, I need some air."

The chair toppled over and clattered to the floor as Hunter made a hasty exit outside. Skye and Camille looked at each other. It wasn't a secret that the Madigan brothers weren't a tightknit group. Hunter wasn't one to share more than he absolutely had to, so for him to reveal this much showed exactly how deep the hurt ran.

"All these boys back in town, and they might as well be gone. Takes more than blood to make a family." Camille sighed and started loading up the dishwasher.

# Chapter Two

Refusing to think about the fracturing of the family who had founded the town, or even worse, the final break between the four brothers, Skye slid down from the chair. "Let's do Hunter a favor and get rid of all these people. They've had their chance to say goodbye to someone they didn't consider a real friend anyway. If they want to gossip further, they can do it somewhere else."

It took a while but between them, Camille and Skye managed to guide everyone out in a way that offended no one. Almost no one. Mrs. Harris sniffed plenty and stuck her nose in the air. The Madigans were nowhere to be found.

"It's still so strange to think that he's just gone," Camille said as she looked around the empty living room. "I know not a lot of people liked him, but Thomas Madigan had his moments. He was a good boss for sure."

Skye put an arm around Camille's shoulders. They'd been best friends for more than a decade, and Camille had been working at The Madigan Sawmill for almost as long. Few people had known the often-brusque Thomas Madigan as well as Camille; like everyone else, he had layers that he'd kept mostly to himself. Sure, he had been nothing but pleasant—in his own way—to Skye over the years. But to Camille, who had grown up without her parents, he had been somewhat of a father figure, whether he had known it or not.

"I liked him." Very much, Skye admitted to herself. "He told me how grateful he was to have you at the mill. Said it'd have been dust in the wind a long time ago without you."

Camille's laugh was shaky. "That old coot."

Hunter came in, stopping short when he saw them. Or maybe it was the lack of people that surprised him. Behind Hunter was one of the city lawyers who had set up shop in town a few years ago.

"We're on our way out," Skye said with a squeeze to Camille's shoulder. "Just reminiscing a little."

He shook his head. "No, please stay. I don't know how you got everyone out, but thank you. I know I should have been more patient, more hospitable, but they just irked me."

"They didn't really care. They were just curious about getting a peek at the house and at y'all together." Camille hastily wiped away a tear from her cheek .

"Yeah." Hunter cleared his throat. "Anyway, we're just...the will, you know. I thought it was best to get it over with today since we're all here and may be scattered again tomorrow. Have you seen my brothers?"

"Not lately, but we'll find them and finish up in the kitchen. Then we'll head out." Skye went over to hug him, her heart breaking for him. Hunter Madigan was the most laidback, steady, self-assured man she had ever known, and in that moment he looked like a strong gust of wind might knock him over.

"Thanks, Skye. And thanks for your help today, Camille. You went above and beyond."

"No, I didn't. I loved him, too." She marched out, leaving Skye to offer Hunter an apologetic shrug and hurry after her.

Camille took kitchen duty, which left Skye to look for the rest of the Madigan brood. She wasn't even sure she actually wanted to find Cameron, but she had promised Hunter she would round up all his brothers. Luckily she found Julian first. He was still on the front porch, curled up in a rocker and looking like he might be asleep.

"Julian?"

"Not interested."

"Not interested in what exactly?" She sat down in the rocker next to his, knocking over one of the empty beer cans underneath it.

"Anything."

"I don't blame you, but there's a lawyer in there, probably on the clock, waiting to read your daddy's will."

Julian snorted and opened his eyes. "And now they expect me to go in there to let the old man rub it in that he's left everything to his one perfect son. No thanks. I should have done like Cam and Reid and left years ago."

"Why didn't you?" Skye didn't know if it had done Cameron and Reid any good to get out of town, but Julian had been miserable for a long time. Maybe leaving could have helped him.

"I had no fancy dream to chase, did I?"

"Everyone has dreams."

"Not me." With less than steady hands, he lit a cigarette.

They sat in silence. Something about Julian often made Skye want to help him somehow, but right then his behavior grated on her nerves a little. Today was for grieving, not pouting because you weren't getting your way.

Reid came up the porch stairs after a few minutes. "Hello, beautiful Skye. Strawberry."

Julian sneered at the old, hated nickname that stemmed back from when he was a toddler with strawberry blond hair and three older brothers just looking for someone to pick on. The unruly, dark blond hair he'd grown into over the years hadn't made the nickname go away.

"Hi, Reid." Skye had talked briefly with the second-youngest Madigan brother earlier and knew he'd sailed into port just this morning on his sailboat and expected to leave again soon, heading off for new adventures beyond the horizon. Reid was never happier than when adrenaline rushed through him, flying across oceans on his little sailboat, diving with sharks, paragliding off steep cliffs, and whatever else gave him his kicks. Those were hard to find in Maeville.

Skye rose. "Hunter's inside with a lawyer."

"Ah, the will. He mentioned that earlier. Well, let's get it over with. Come on, Straw."

Grumbling, Julian rose and knocked over more empty beer cans in the process. He dropped the cigarette and ground it into the wood with his heel.

Reid looked at Skye. "Is Cam inside, too?"

"No. I'll look for him."

"I can do it. I mean, if you'd rather not…"

Skye smiled. "It's okay. I'll find him."

Reid and Julian went inside, and Skye followed her hunch and went around to the back of the house. She walked down the slope beyond the back yard, in between the trees until she reached the river. Instinctively she knew she would find Cameron there.

\* \* \* \*

The temperamental river he shared a name with had always been Cameron's favorite place to escape to growing up. A good place to dream, and an even better place to hide. No matter the season, its beauty could take his breath away, not entirely unlike Skye Jones who was making her way toward him through the trees. Beautiful Skye Jones. She had torn him to shreds just by breathing, made him question himself and everything he had ever wanted. He had dreamed of Nashville and saved for an engagement ring at the same time, not knowing which part of his heart to follow. The day he left, engagement ring in his pocket, he still hadn't known what he wanted more—Skye or to become a star. So he had told himself that he would go and make something of himself first, then come back for her. He never had, of course.

Returning to Maeville, he had known he was bound to see her again. Maybe he had even known the first time would be by the river that had been the backdrop to their romance. They had started dating in high school, and their love had burned bright for almost ten years. In the years that had passed since, Cameron had often thought back and wondered how he had been able to leave her for something as fickle as a dream.

She still wore her black hair long. Cameron knew how soft it was and yearned to touch it. She always moved as if she had all the time in the world, graceful as a nymph, and eyes as green as the deepest forest. Her smile…oh, lord, her smile.

He'd clean forgotten how the slow curving of her lips, and warmth rising as slow as the sunrise in her eyes had the power to bring him to his knees. From a distance, she looked like the young woman he'd left behind, but when she came closer, he could see some of the stars had burned out.

"Hello, Cameron."

There was smoke in her voice. He'd always though it the sexiest voice he'd ever heard, even encouraged her to sing although she had always refused. He had also thought it was embedded in his memory, but he hadn't done her justice. It sounded so much sexier than he remembered.

"Skye. You look fantastic."

"I'm not sure I like the surprise in your voice."

"I didn't mean…"

She smiled. "I'm sure you didn't. So, how's Nashville?"

Cameron stuck his hands in his pockets. "Fine. It's…fine. I'm working on a new album, so…yeah, it's fine."

"I'm glad to hear it. Listen, I'm really sorry about your daddy. It's such a shock."

"Thanks." He'd heard the sentiment repeated quite a few times between the time he had entered the house and escaped out back before the walls closed in on him, but it was different coming from Skye. She was probably the only one who actually meant them. "I don't even know what happened exactly. Hunter called while I was working…in the studio, I mean, and sent a text when I didn't pick up."

Skye came closer, laid a hand on his arm. The simple touch warmed him up inside, making him think he had been ice cold for six years. "He had a stroke. Hunter found him. Camille said he'd been feeling fine that day, so it came out of the blue."

Cameron nodded, trying to focus on her words rather than her touch. It was difficult. And though he understood the words, they seemed to be impossible to apply to Thomas Madigan. "She still working at the mill?" he asked instead.

"Yes." She squeezed his arm. "Cam, I came to find you for Hunter. Your brothers and a lawyer are waiting inside to read the will."

Without meaning to, he pulled his arm away from her touch. "I don't need to be there for that. Hunter, and maybe Straw, will get it all. Daddy never hid his opinion of Reid and me leaving town. Abandoning the family legacy, I think he called it."

"I don't know anything about that, but at least go inside. Catch up with your brothers, mourn together. Just don't leave before you've had a chance to talk."

He stared at her. "I've got nothing to say."

"I don't believe that."

Cameron didn't argue although he couldn't think of a single thing to say to any of his brothers. Clearly he had already failed with Hunter, and Reid's enthusiastic hug earlier hadn't been followed by meaningful conversation. He still hadn't seen Straw.

Yet, after following Skye back to the house, fifteen minutes later he found himself in the company of his brothers and the lawyer. Cameron discovered that the drunk on the front porch was, in fact, his youngest brother.

He had been a kid when Cam left town, and apparently he had only changed in appearance, because he still acted very much like a sullen kid. A drunk one.

"I won't keep you long," the lawyer told them from the head of the massive dining room table, where he presided with his fancy briefcase and twinkling cufflinks. "Your father changed his last will and testament about two years ago, and he was very precise in his wishes. The majority of what he owned, including this house, the land, the sawmill, the money, is to be divided equally between you as his sons. A small amount is set aside for a Miss Camille Bradford."

Cameron wasn't sure he was able to conceal his surprise. The last thing his daddy had told him, six years earlier while Cameron was putting the last of his belongings in his truck, was that turning your back on the family legacy had consequences. Cameron had figured it meant that he was on his own. No contact, no love, no inheritance.

"Your inheritance, however, comes with a condition," the lawyer, whose name Cameron hadn't caught, continued. "If it's not met, everything, save for the amount earmarked for Miss Bradford, will go to Hunter."

Straw laughed, an ugly laugh without mirth. "Here it comes. Should have known."

"Shut up," Hunter told him, the steely look in his eyes clashing with his weary posture.

"Easy for you to say, isn't it? You get it all."

Hunter rubbed his forehead and looked away when his gaze met Cameron's across the table. "Please continue, Mr. Kane."

The lawyer cleared his throat. "The condition is that you are all to live in this house and work at the sawmill for one year from today. If you do that, live together, work together, and keep the sawmill the healthy business it is now, you each inherit one fourth of your father's estate. If you fail to meet this condition, even if just one of you fails to meet it—and I should mention that I've been charged with keeping an eye on you—Hunter inherits everything. Those are your father's wishes. Let it sink in, and if you have any questions, I'll leave my card so you can get in touch with me."

Hunter showed the lawyer out. Cameron was still busy analyzing his own feelings when Straw stood abruptly, sending his chair clattering into the cabinet behind him. He started pacing.

"Shit. We dump the old man into the ground, and he still fucks up our lives. There was no pleasing him, still isn't apparently. Shit. I stayed. I fucking stayed, and what does that get me? Nothing. You guys ran first chance you got, but I stayed like Hunter."

Reid rose, too, and headed for the liquor cabinet. "One last drink on the old man's tab. It's the least he can do."

"How about showing him some respect?" Hunter marched in and poured a cup of coffee from the loaded tray on the table. "You buried your daddy today. Does that mean nothing to you?"

"I think I buried my daddy six years ago." The surge of temper in Cameron's chest that had risen at the lawyer's words disappeared, and he joined Reid in front of the liquor cabinet. He hoped a drink or two would conjure it back—anger was preferable to the other emotions welling up in his chest.

"That's your own fault." Hunter picked up his coffee cup with a jerky movement that made the hot liquid spill onto his hand. With a muttered curse, he put the cup back down.

"Why don't you get off his back?" Straw's pacing had taken him around the table a few times, and he stopped in front of Hunter. "You've already gotten it all. The moment of glory for the golden son, who can do no wrong."

"Didn't you listen to what Mr. Kane said? Or were you too drunk, hungover, or stoned? It's only mine if you ungrateful assholes make it mine. Daddy didn't leave me more than he's left y'all, quite the opposite in fact. He gave you a choice, in case you hadn't noticed."

Straw snorted. "Some choice. Endure hell or get nothing. Thanks, Daddy."

"I think it was clever," Reid said, sitting down with his tumbler of whiskey. "He wanted Hunter to have it all, but had to make it look like he was at least giving the rest of us a chance. He gets his way but makes it seem as if it's our decision. Man was a lot of things, but he wasn't dumb, our daddy. Cheers."

Cameron had no way of knowing if Reid was right or not. Part of him thought that he probably was, but it didn't change that they all had a choice.

Sure, he couldn't imagine the four of them living and working together either, but the choice was there nonetheless. Cameron had gotten so used to crappy choices that this didn't seem very much out of the ordinary. That, however, didn't take away the anger or the sense of betrayal.

Yes, he'd left. Yes, Reid had left. It didn't make them worth any less that they had gone beyond the outer limits of Maeville to pursue their dreams. And Straw had stayed, so why the hell was he getting screwed over? Cameron couldn't decide whether to wash his hands of the whole thing and just leave, or dig in and say *screw you* to the old man.

He'd been lost in thought in front of the liquor cabinet, and Straw came over to nudge him out of the way. As his younger brother searched for the bottle he wanted, Cameron got his first real good look at him up close. Straw looked terrible—unshaven, pale, with dark circles marring the skin under his eyes. His hair was a holy mess, and he reeked of stale beer and cigarette smoke.

"Don't you think you've had enough?"

Straw turned his head. "Just because Daddy's dead doesn't mean you have to start acting like a big brother. My life's been fine without you in it for the past six years, and it will continue to be so long after you've galloped back out of town on your high horse."

"Better than being the town drunk." The anger Cameron had been wishing would return finally made an appearance. He stalked across the room to glare out the window. "Is it so hard to understand that some of us had dreams that took us beyond town borders? Good Lord."

"You tell 'em, brother."

Cameron turned to scowl at Reid. "You're already on your way out the door, so why don't you shut up?"

Reid stood. "And you're not? Oh, come on. You've always thought you were better than the rest of us, Mr. Country Music Star. I'd like to see you leave your cushy life in Nashville to slave away at the sawmill and bunk with your brothers again."

The shards of the dream that had shattered inside Cameron years ago drove their pointy edges into his heart once again. He saw Straw stalking over and starting to yell something. Even Hunter joined in on the heated argument that quickly turned into pushing and shoving. But Cameron heard nothing. Felt nothing. He just knew his vision was going hazy, and if he didn't get some fresh air and some space, he'd keel over.

So he bolted.

# Chapter Three

The evening air was cool, but Skye was restless and hoped a nice, long walk would do her good. She had stopped by the clinic on her way home from the Madigan house and filled her curious father in on the happenings at the funeral. Mostly he had been interested in whether she had seen and talked to Cameron, which had irked her a little. Then she'd had dinner with a preoccupied Camille, who was taking her boss' death hard but refused to talk about it. Skye would wait her out, though.

Earlier, she had known she would find Cameron at the river. Now she once more found herself heading toward the waters that had given life to the town, only she had her own favorite spot a little further west than the Madigan house in mind. The river ran straighter here, rushing by, and she had solved many problems and wrestled with herself many times beside the old, rickety wooden bridge that had long ago fallen out of use.

Though he had been on her mind, and most likely was the reason she was so restless if she bothered admitting it to herself, Skye had not expected to run into Cameron again. But there he was, huddled against the remnants of the old bridge, staring out over the water. Part of Skye wanted to turn back before he saw her, but her legs kept walking despite her mind's reservations.

"Cameron."

He jolted at the sound of her voice, then visibly relaxed. "Hey, sugar."

Once upon a time she had all but melted every time Cameron Madigan called her *sugar*. It wasn't so much the common term of endearment as the way his lips curved up slightly whenever he said it, looking at her as if she was the center of the universe. Whether his lips had curved this time, she didn't know, poor light and distance against her, but her heart fluttered all the same.

"What are you doing here?"

He pushed away from the bridge and shrugged. "Just walking. Ended up here, I guess. Remember how we used to dare each other to walk across the bridge when we were kids? Straw was always too scared."

"And six years younger than you."

"Kid had to keep up or get left behind." Cameron sighed. "What the hell happened to him?"

Skye didn't play dumb, as much as she wanted to. It was the town's worst kept secret that Julian Madigan was headed down the wrong path, but Cameron had no way of knowing since he had been gone for so long. "The polite way of saying it is that Julian still hasn't found a proper outlet for all the anger he has inside of him. He's gotten mixed up with a bad crowd, drinks too much, sneers at anyone who wants to help. I don't know what happened between him and your daddy, but they weren't talking much. He's hurting, Cam. I don't know why."

"Fucking kid."

"Maybe that's exactly why he's hurting, or at least part of it. *Fucking kid.* Strawberry. Nobody in his family takes him seriously. Even your daddy, bless his soul, called him Straw. He hates that nickname so much."

Cameron held up his palms. "Excuse me. I didn't know you'd become a Madigan expert in my absence."

"I'm sorry to disappoint you, but your family didn't turn their backs on me when you did. Hunter's a good friend, Julian too when he lets me. I cared a great deal for your daddy."

"Those who stayed stick together."

"It's hard to stick to someone who leaves you."

"I didn't...shit, Skye. I didn't leave *you.*"

She laughed tiredly. It had been a long day, and she imagined the day had been even longer for Cameron. "You left me high and dry. You can spin yarns all day about dreams, dreams we shared by the way, Cam, but the fact is that you left me. You left your family, your friends, your home, and you left *me.*"

"I had to."

"Not the way you did. You weren't a teenager; you were an adult. And so was I. The least I deserved was an explanation. I hope Nashville is worth it." The moment the words left her mouth, she regretted them a little. She knew they would sting. On the other hand, it had more than stung when Cameron had left.

"You didn't come after me. You could have."

Skye nodded. It was getting dark now, and she had trouble seeing him clearly. Soon she would have trouble seeing the path back home. "Sure I could. I could have come begging for your attention, your love, after you'd left me in the dust. Absolutely. But I didn't. Dignity was pretty much all I had left, so I didn't feel like throwing it out the window for someone who didn't give a damn."

"So you gave up on your dreams?"

She balled up her fists, nails digging into her palms. "Screw your *dreams*, Cameron Madigan. They're nothing but lies unless you make them come true."

Skye didn't often stalk off angrily, maybe because she had lived in a nice, peaceful town many, many miles from Cameron. He certainly had that effect on her, she fumed to herself as she struggled to see the path in front of her. Had he always been so insufferable? So high and almighty, basing everything he said and thought on decade-old dreams?

"Skye, wait!"

She could hear him behind her, but she didn't stop. As much as she would have liked to have a normal conversation, that was obviously off the table.

"Dammit."

Reaching the road, she glanced over her shoulder and saw him through the trees. "Go home, Cameron. Goodnight."

He didn't follow her farther, and Skye walked briskly home. To think she had taken a walk to get the restlessness out of her body. What a joke.

\* \* \* \*

Were dreams that didn't come true nothing more than lies? Cameron contemplated it on his way back to the house. He hadn't meant to stay away for so long, but he had gotten caught up in his own thoughts. Now he was cold, starving, and no more ready to face his brothers and the battle that waited than he had been when he stormed out earlier.

Lights were on at the house. To a frozen, hungry man, they almost seemed welcoming. But a frozen, hungry man might also be hallucinating. Cameron went around back and let himself in through the backdoor, not at all sure he was welcome, but too tired to care.

He shed his jacket and his hat, heading straight for the fridge. It was filled to the brim with dishes and casseroles, and he grabbed the first one handy and shoved it in the oven.

Somewhere in the house, someone was talking or watching TV. With no interest in figuring out which, Cameron dug out a beer. Although he had spent hours walking by the river thinking about it, he still didn't have the faintest idea what on earth his daddy had thought writing his will. Thomas Madigan hadn't been a family man, but he had liked to be perceived as one. Appearances mattered, which was probably why he had thought it looked less than stellar to have two of his sons leave town, hot on the trail of dreams he had thought very little of. *Music isn't a career for real men*, he had told Cameron. *Sailing is something you do on vacation* had been the message for Reid. And yet, when he'd had the chance to cut them both off completely, he hadn't done it.

Fatherly love maybe, Cameron thought to himself as he sat down at the kitchen table with a steaming plate of Shepherd's Pie. Though his daddy hadn't done much in ways of showing that fatherly love when he was alive, so why now? Perhaps it was to mess with them. Show them that although he gave them the chance, they would muck up working and living together. One last chance stick it to them from the grave that they had no idea how to be a family.

Reid wandered in, draining the last sip of beer out of a can. He came over to sniff at Cameron's meal. "Anymore of that?"

"On the counter."

"Sweet."

Growing up, Cameron had always been closer to Hunter than to Reid and Straw. Probably because they were closer in age. These days, Cameron had more in common with Reid, who had felt the same chill directed at him for leaving Maeville, the center of the universe to its inhabitants. Although, as they ate in awkward silence, it was clear they had nothing much in common after all.

"You cool off?" Reid asked, getting up to get a second helping.

"In more ways than one."

Reid snickered. "Straw tore out of here not long after you. Hunter's brooding. So what do you reckon the old man was thinking?"

Cameron rose and went to rinse off his plate. "The old man always liked to get in the last word. Seems to me that's what he's doing now."

"If it's that important to him, he can have it. I've got a tide to catch in the morning."

Cameron turned. "You're leaving?"

"Yeah, sure. Aren't you?"

"Well, I…I don't know. I haven't decided."

"Why would you want to give up your career to come back here and slave away at the mill?"

"I don't know that I would, but I think we should at least give it one serious conversation."

"Good luck with that. Straw's so mad I'm surprised the top of his head hasn't blown off already, and Hunter's got no interest in us sticking around."

"And you?" Cameron asked, leaning back against the counter and watching Reid. He'd always been the adventurous one, climbing one limb higher in the trees, staying out half an hour longer, swimming out further in the river than the rest of them. Pinning him to one place for an extended period of time had always been difficult, even if it had just been for a class in school or a family dinner.

"This place isn't for me, Cam. I need wide open spaces and endless oceans. Miles and miles of water beneath the hull of the boat, wind in my hair. Not sawdust and stifling town gossip."

Cameron nodded. He didn't understand the need to be on the water, but he understood the need to follow a dream, and he definitely understood needing to get out of Maeville.

Reid rose with his plate in his hand and shrugged. "But if we can swing it, I'll do that one serious conversation. I guess we owe each other at least that. Or owe Daddy."

"Thanks," Cameron felt compelled to say. When Reid left, he stared out of the window for a while, seeing nothing but the darkness and wondering what, if anything at all, that one serious conversation would result in. A lot hinged on it going well.

After dealing with the dishes, Cameron wandered through the house. It was comforting in its timeless, hardly-ever-changing way. Family heirlooms treasured by generations of Madigans, furniture Cameron could remember curling up on as a kid. It would all be Hunter's the moment just one of them left. His fate, Cameron realized, was balancing in the unsteady hands of an adventurer itching to leave and an angry kid who didn't seem to know what he wanted.

"You're back."

Cameron had wandered into his daddy's office and hadn't noticed Hunter sitting behind the massive oak desk.

His eyes had been on the painting above the fireplace. He had always loved it, been comforted many times as a boy to see his pretty great-great-great-grandmother smiling down with her Mona Lisa smile.

"Yeah."

"Too bad Straw's gone."

"Yep."

Hunter sighed and closed the book in front of him on the desk. "I wish y'all would just make an effort."

"We'll talk tomorrow. That's soon enough," Cameron said, trying to keep his temper in check. It seemed to bubble up every time he attempted to talk with Hunter.

Rubbing his forehead, Hunter rose and put the book on a shelf behind the desk. "Yeah, it's soon enough. I called Mr. Kane again to clarify a few things. He said we could take a few days to decide."

"Great." He had already turned to walk out, but he looked back over his shoulder. Hunter's forehead was pressed against a row of books on a shelf, and something inside Cameron constricted painfully. "Hey, Hunt? I'm sorry about Daddy."

He saw Hunter nod, and then he left the office. Since no one had officially left yet—from what he'd heard, he figured Straw was just out getting drunk and in trouble—he decided it would be okay to stay the night at the house. Their house for one more night, then all Hunter's.

Detouring outside to his car for his stuff, he headed toward his old room. For all he knew, it had been converted into storage years ago. So he was more than just a little surprised to see that it looked pretty much untouched. Well, not untouched. It was clean, but all the things he'd left behind were still there. He had moved out when he was around twenty, but the little cabin out near the mill where he had lived hadn't been big enough to hold all his things. So he had kept some at the house, occasionally spending a night there.

Too tired after a long day to do much more than shed his clothes, he slid gratefully in between the sheets. It felt so familiar that he almost expected Straw to turn up the music down the hall and his daddy to come hollering to keep the noise down. But, of course, that would never happen again. His daddy was dead, something that hadn't hit as hard before as it did right then.

\* \* \* \*

"Yes, it was, Mrs. Roberts." Skye noted down the woman's blood pressure and offered what she dubbed her professional smile—the one that she could manage even when she would rather have her toenails pulled off with pliers. She should have known she was in for a day where the patients could talk about nothing but Thomas Madigan's final sendoff.

"Just a darn shame that none of the boys' mommas were there. Would have been a nice gesture."

"It would. I think the doctor is ready for you now, Mrs. Roberts. Go on right through."

Skye updated the electronic chart and grabbed a cup of coffee. A lot could be said about the Madigans, but they didn't give local gossipers more fodder than absolutely necessary. Well, except Julian of course. Mrs. Roberts' comment about the Madigan brothers' mommas had been innocent enough if you didn't know what Skye knew. It was common knowledge that Cameron's momma had died giving birth to him. Mr. Madigan and his second wife, Hunter's momma, had divorced. Estelle had moved to Raleigh, and they had bounced Hunter back and forth for a while until he had finally gotten old enough to say that he didn't like the city and would rather live with his daddy on the edge of the forest by the river. He had kept in contact with his momma, though, up until her death a little over a year ago. That was not common knowledge in Maeville.

Reid's momma had the same adventurer gene that she had passed onto her son. She and Mr. Madigan hadn't gotten married, and she had jetted off on her next expedition when Reid was just a baby, though she had never severed contact with him. Then there was Julian's momma. Skye sneered into her coffee cup. Julian never mentioned her, but Hunter had told Skye enough for her to hate the woman. The third Mrs. Madigan was currently on marriage number four and had left Julian as effectively as she had left Julian's daddy. Skye suspected a lot of Julian's anger stemmed from the horrid woman who had given birth to him. And who could blame him?

Draining the last of her coffee, she sighed. The patients talked about the Madigans, and she thought about them when she should be working. A glance at the appointment book told her that the Jacobs twins were due in for their inoculations. That ought to keep her focused on work. They were terrors in diapers.

"Lots of talk of the Madigans today," Skye's dad commented over lunch in their little break room at the clinic.

The Jacobs twins had given her a headache, and she hoped lunch would cure it. She nodded as she stabbed her fork into the container with fruit salad.

"Irks me that I couldn't attend the funeral myself."

"By now you've heard all there is to hear about it from the patients and from me."

Her daddy nodded as he bit into his sandwich. "Probably," he allowed a moment later. "But I liked Tom Madigan. It would have been nice to show him a last respect. We might not have been friends, I doubt anyone held that title with him, but I liked him well enough. And I've known him since we were boys."

"It's hard to live in a town the size of Maeville without knowing someone one way or the other."

"It is. I think I'll stop by the Madigan house and pay my respect to the boys later. Lord knows they're hard enough to pin down in the same spot."

"Hunter will appreciate that."

"But not the others?"

Skye looked at her daddy and shrugged. "I don't know. I know Hunter and the kind of man he is, but the others… I just don't know. Cam's been gone for six years, Reid's been mostly gone for a decade, and Julian…he might be here, but he doesn't want to be. I don't know them anymore."

"You said you talked to Cameron. Has he really changed that much?"

"It seems like it. Don't be too hard on him, though. Whether he's realized it or not, he's grieving."

"So were you when he left," her daddy pointed out.

"Cam didn't die. He just left."

"The end result was the same. He wasn't here."

"That was his choice, Daddy. We don't have to like it, but it was his to make."

Her daddy rose after finishing his lunch. "You're sweet as a peach, honey, but your momma and I should have taught you to hold a grudge. It's good for the soul sometimes."

Skye wasn't so sure that she didn't still hold a grudge against Cameron, but she was, however, sure it did the soul absolutely no good.

The afternoon passed with patients and more talk about the Madigans. Cameron's return was, not surprisingly, the hottest topic.

"You know, I never did understand why Thomas Madigan made such a fuss about young Cameron going off to make his music. His only crime was to leave the way he did. Well, you'd know, Skye."

Skye offered her polite smile to Lottie Winters, who had run the local bakery and gossip central longer than Skye could recall.

"And that Julian. Always raising hell with those friends of his. I think I'd have keeled over and died, too, if I had a boy like that."

Even the polite smile slipped at that, and Skye might have, accidentally, of course, jabbed the needle with the flu vaccine in with a little more force than strictly necessary.

# Chapter Four

Cameron ate breakfast alone. He had no idea where his brothers were, but the half pot of lukewarm coffee suggested that at least one of them had been up before him. He wondered if Straw still lived at home, if Reid had somewhere else he stayed when he was in town. He had cut those ties himself over the years. Not right off. He had been decent at e-mailing and calling the first year or so. Then...it had simply become easier not to. And no one else had been interested in keeping in contact either.

Once he had eaten, Cameron didn't know what to do with himself. Both annoyed that no one else was around and grateful that he was alone—he still didn't know how to approach the situation—he ended up doing laundry. He had a pile of it in his car, and it was nice to get it done without being holed up at a Laundromat.

Reid wandered in just before lunch, smelling like the motor oil he was wearing on his face. "Been messing with my boat's emergency engine. It's been acting up since the Los Roques Islands," he said in explanation to Cameron's no doubt puzzled look before heading for the shower.

Lunch appeared to be the unspoken meeting time. Hunter came in, carting three grocery bags and the smell of freshly cut wood. As much as Cameron had despised it in the past, it was the smell of his childhood. It was clear that Hunter had been working all morning. His sweater was full of wood chips, and little blobs of sap clung to his cargo pants.

"Straw's on his way. Reid here?"

"In the shower," Cameron replied before getting up to help Hunter with the groceries. He still remembered where everything went in the cupboards, and got the oddest feeling in his chest when he realized it. Growing up, they'd all had specific chores, and for years putting groceries away had been one of his. Remembering made him nostalgic, and not all in a bad way.

"Good. I don't have all day for this, so I figured we could eat while talking. Some of us have a job to get back to." Hunter started making grilled cheese sandwiches, stopping only to make an irritated gesture toward a cupboard. Cameron got it. Tomato soup. That was his job, and had been a million times before in a distant past where he and Hunter had been in charge of cooking. It had taken them years to add a second dish to their cooking repertoire.

Reid came downstairs with wet hair and a t-shirt slung over his bare shoulder. Without saying anything, he started setting the table. They had yet to prove that they could say more than a few sentences to each other without arguing, but making lunch together was a good start. Straw, however, just had to ruin it. He came in and sat down at the table without a word. He lit a cigarette and used one of the soup bowls as an ashtray.

Reid muttered under his breath and grabbed another bowl from the cupboard. Cameron blocked his way to the table, shaking his head when Reid started to object. Smiling pleasantly — he hadn't worked as a waiter in vain — Cameron looked over at Straw. "If it's not too much trouble," he drawled with barely-concealed impatience," think you could grab us a few drinks from the fridge in the pantry?"

Straw shrugged, but rose and disappeared from the kitchen, the cigarette dangling between his fingers.

Cameron took the pot of hot soup and went over to the table to fill the bowls. All the bowls.

Reid snickered.

Cameron sat down, looking expectantly at Reid until he did the same. A moment later, Hunter joined them with a big plate of grilled cheese, and Straw came back with beers and a lone Coke for Hunter, which was delivered with an eye-roll. Drinking during the workday was not permitted at the mill, Cameron recalled clearly.

More than once he'd seen what happened when people didn't follow that very basic rule. For reasons he couldn't explain even to himself, he got up to grab a glass of water and ignored both the beer and the curious look Hunter sent him.

The silence stretched awkwardly as they started to eat. Straw dug into his soup and ate about half before he abruptly pushed it away and glared across the table at Cameron.

"Nice. Real damn nice. Fucker."

Cameron smirked. "Karma's a bitch, little brother."

"If y'all aren't going to start, I might as well do it," Hunter said, and Cameron could hear the implied "*like I do everything else*" at the end. "Daddy wanted us to become a family again, and his way was to force us to stick together for a while. I don't know if that's the right way or not, but I hope you'll stay for Daddy's sake. And, I guess, for my sake. Not just because I can't handle all the work at the mill myself, but because I miss how it used to be. How we used to be."

"You could hire people," Reid pointed out. "You gain nothing by having us stay, quite the opposite. You lose seventy-five percent of your inheritance."

Hunter shook his head. "I inherit twenty-five percent just like each of you. I only inherit more if you throw yours away."

"Easy for you to say." Reid drained his beer. "You don't have to give anything up. You just continue on with your life just the way you like it."

"That's true. But I can't change the will anymore than you can. We can all just try to get the best out of the last thing Daddy's asked of us."

"Asked?" Straw sneered. "Daddy never *asked* anything. He demanded. Even from the grave he's demanding things to be done his way or not at all. It's bullshit."

Hunter rolled his eyes. "So is your attitude."

"Seems to me there are two hurdles in this," Cameron said, thinking out loud. "One is whether or not to actually do it. Weigh the pros and the cons. The second is making it work. If we can't get through lunch without disagreeing, living together and running the mill together for a year will be impossible."

"Don't worry about that. Hunter will boss us around at the mill and give us chores and curfews here at home," Straw said, lighting another cigarette.

"And tell you that you should go outside if you want to get lung cancer," Reid added.

Hunter rose. "I can't tell you what to decide and what to do. Won't. But I hope you stay. I'll be out at the mill."

Silence fell again after Hunter left. Cameron had a hard time pinning down his thoughts as they buzzed around in his head. More and more, the idea of staying appealed to him. Having a real home again, a steady job, a family. Roots.

Working at the sawmill had never been what he wanted, not before anyway. Now, after the last six years in Nashville, he was less picky. He had never imagined himself returning to Maeville either, but he had done a lot of things he had never imagined he would do. Coming home to stay didn't seem so outlandish anymore. Besides, if he didn't like it, he could always reevaluate when the year was up.

Reid sighed. "I might go crazy being stuck on land for so long, but if y'all want me to stay, I will. One of us bailing will ruin it for the others. I can try to stick it out for a year."

"Don't go doing anyone any favors," Straw sneered.

"I'll stay, too," Cameron said, ignoring Straw. "I don't know if I want to work at the sawmill or even stay in Maeville for the rest of my life, but I'd like to see what it's like. I can stick it out for a year, too."

Reid rose and started to rinse off plates and bowls. "What about your career?"

"It'll keep."

Reid looked at him with a frown, and Cameron quickly averted his gaze. He didn't want to go into details. "Straw?"

"What? Do I want to give up my big career, my big, sprawling mansion, my exotic lifestyle, and move in here to bunk with my condescending brothers for a year, slave away at the blasted mill that I spent years trying to escape from? Sure. Because that's what *you* want, what Daddy wanted."

Cameron shook his head. It was all down to a brat with a big chip on his shoulder now. "I'm asking you what you want. You're free to make whatever choice you think is best for you."

* * * *

There were seven missed calls on Skye's cellphone when she locked up the clinic and headed home late that afternoon. They were all from Camille, and she called again before Skye had a chance to listen to the voicemails.

"Hey. Where's the fire?"

"At the sawmill. The place is ablaze with Madigan tension if not actual flames. You're not going to believe it, Skye."

"Believe what?" Skye waved to a couple of people she knew before turning away from Main Street and heading toward her cabin on the edge of town.

"Hunter's at work, obviously," Camille said. "But not long after lunch, Cameron, Reid, and Julian showed up, too. They're working. Cam and Reid are poking about in the furniture workshop, and Julian's bagging woodchips between loud bouts of complaining that he can't smoke here. Do you know what's going on?"

"I haven't the faintest idea. I thought Cam and Reid would be on their way back out of town by now."

"Me too." Camille cleared her throat. "I wonder if..."

"If what?"

"Well, we reckoned Mr. Madigan would leave everything to Hunter, or at least only to Hunter and Julian. But what if he didn't? What if he forgave Cameron and Reid and left the sawmill to all of them? Though, that doesn't explain why Cam would give up his career in Nashville and Reid abandon the sea."

"Maybe they're just taking a few days to spend together. No matter who inherits the mill, you guys are a man down over there without Mr. Madigan. They could just be pitching in for the day."

It was easier to tell herself that anyway. It was easier without Cameron around to remind her of what they'd had together, but she still hated the thought of him leaving again. And she'd be damned if she started getting her hopes up about him staying just to have them ground into dust a second time.

"Maybe." Camille's tone made it clear that she wasn't convinced, and her worry gene had kicked in. Camille worried about everyone, took care of the people she loved whether they thought they needed it or not.

"One of us is bound to get the truth out of Hunter eventually," Skye said.

"Hunter's a closed book."

"No, he isn't. He just takes a little coercing to get something out of."

"A lot."

"Okay, okay." Skye grinned. "But we'll make him talk."

"He's a frustrating man."

Entertained by the thought, the smile stayed fixed on Skye's face even when it started raining. "I think he's one of the most straightforward men I've ever met."

"That's because he's your ex-boyfriend's brother, thus firmly placed in the friend zone. To me, he's...well, frustrating."

"Camille, this is news. He's not in the friend zone with you?"

"I don't know. And I shouldn't have said anything. It's nothing, really."

"You wouldn't have brought it up if it was nothing." Skye lengthened her stride as the rain increased.

"We've had some…encounters, I guess you could call them. He asked me out last week, but someone yelled for him before I could reply, then we got busy, and Hunter went home to find his daddy…you know. He hasn't brought it up again, but if he does, what do I say? He's my boss now."

"You're afraid to blur the lines?" Skye asked. She had never considered the thought of Camille and Hunter, never suspected they had either. She was unsure of the match, but knew better than anyone that the heart wanted what the heart wanted.

"Yes, because I love my job. No, because it's Hunter for mercy's sake. I don't know, okay? But he's on his way in now, so I gotta go. Bye."

Skye pocketed her phone and ran the last half-mile home. Camille hid so much of her personality. Not deliberately, Skye suspected, but because she wasn't sure people would like what was underneath the top layers. Or because she just didn't want to share. Now Skye couldn't help but wonder what straight-laced, what-you-see-is-what-you-get Hunter would think if he knew Camille the way Skye did. In any case, wondering about Camille and Hunter was safer than entertaining thoughts about why Cameron was suddenly working at the sawmill, a place he had always proclaimed to detest.

\* \* \* \*

Cameron's muscles cried for mercy — wailed, actually — but he wasn't about to admit it to anyone. He had only been at it a few hours, anyway. He used to be able to work full days at the mill and barely feel it.

Nashville had made him soft. Pride and a strange feeling of excitement made him push on. Straw had grudgingly said he would try to stick it out for the year, too, but that he wasn't promising anything. His language hadn't been quite as polite, but Reid and Cameron had gotten the gist of it. They were all in. And since they were, they had headed out to tell Hunter and to get started on their yearlong sentence.

Hunter obviously wanted them to stay to honor their daddy's memory, appearing not to care that he would inherit everything on his own if just one of them bailed. Reid wasn't particularly interested in what happened at all. Cameron understood Straw as little as he understood himself. His youngest brother was angry with the world and everyone in it, which was not news. Straw had always been angry, and he certainly hadn't cheered up in the past six years. As for Cameron himself, he wasn't ready to admit exactly why he had decided to stay. He had gotten good at lying, even to himself, so he could pretend, at least for a while, that he was doing it for different reasons than the real ones.

He turned off the circular saw and drank greedily from the bottle of water at his feet.

Straw wandered over, not overly enthusiastic about bagging wood chips. "This sucks."

"It's honest work."

"Says the big country star. What the hell are you doing here, man? You could be on stage in Nashville, having chicks throw their panties at you and flashing their tits."

"Would you believe that I'd rather listen to your foul language?"

"No."

"And people say you're not smart. Let's put it down to responsibility."

"To Daddy?" The sneer was back in Straw's voice.

"To Daddy, to myself, to you, Hunter, and Reid."

"How noble of you. I guess it's true that all the big stars give to charity. Next time you can just send a check, though."

"Is that what you dream about, Strawberry? Getting checks for doing nothing? If so, you're in the wrong place." Cameron started the saw back up, the noise drowning out any reply Straw might have had. Seconds later he stomped off like a kid throwing a tantrum.

Finding a rhythm in the work despite his aching arms and shoulders, Cameron let his thoughts wander. It was easy to go back six or seven years in his head to a time where he had been standing at this exact saw and wished for the workday to be over. He had wanted away from the sawmill, spending the evenings with Skye building castles in the air. He had also wanted out of Maeville, and eventually he'd gotten what he wanted. He and Skye had talked about it for years, ever since high school.

Nashville had always been their dream destination. Cameron wanted to be on stage, Skye wanted to write music. But then, as he had begun to finalize plans, she had enrolled in nursing school. She had kept saying she still wanted to write her music and come with him to Nashville.

At first he'd believed her, used some of the money he had been saving to buy her a ring. They would be the power couple of Nashville. Then, after a while, he'd started to convince himself that her heart wasn't in it. Her passion for writing music didn't burn as brightly after she cut back on her waitressing shifts and started training as a nurse. The ring had stayed in his pocket, and he hadn't asked her to come when he left for Nashville.

Maybe it had been pride, maybe it had been hurt that she'd given up on their dream. Maybe he hadn't been as confident about how he would do in Nashville, or maybe he had just simply been afraid she would say no. Whatever the reason, he hadn't handled leaving very well. Pride had gotten in the way of telling her properly, explaining, even saying goodbye.

And he had second-guessed himself all the way to the country music capital. Maybe his guilty conscience had been the reason for the work rage he had thrown himself headfirst into. It was certainly the reason he'd only sent home postcards. They didn't leave a lot of room for details or for explaining.

He wondered if there was a way to make it up to her. She definitely deserved it. It had been a jolt to the system to see her the previous day. Over and over, when the longing was too strong, he had told himself that his mind was playing tricks on him. There was no way she could be as beautiful, her smile as enchanting, her eyes as green as his memory conjured up. And it had been true. His memory hadn't done her half as much justice as she deserved.

That led to thoughts of what she had been doing in the past six years. Who she'd been with. Who she *was* with. It was agonizing to think about. Not more than he deserved, but still. Although he had turned his back on everyone in town, there had to be someone he could ask, someone who didn't mind sharing the local gossip. Problem was that he didn't know where to start without stirring up gossip himself after being gone for so long.

# Chapter Five

Most days, Skye loved working at the medical clinic with her daddy. He had been the only doctor in town longer than she could remember, and he had no plans of retiring. Her momma had been his nurse until Skye graduated, by then choosing to retire and embrace her passion for painting. These days, watercolors were filling up the house Skye had grown up in.

Her work meant that she knew or knew of most of the people in town, which she usually enjoyed. Three days of people trying to get a reaction out of her about the return of Cameron Madigan was almost more than she could take, though. Everyone knew the story of the oldest Madigan boy and Doc's Skye. How it had blossomed, how it had ended. Of course, no one knew exactly how much she had been hurt or how much they were hurting her now by not letting her forget, or at least ignore, that he was back—and that she had a strong suspicion he could still hurt her as much as ever.

Skye sighed and took inventory of the waiting room. Mr. Evans was in for a diabetes check-up, Mary Solomon was scheduled for a sonogram, and...her eyes met Cameron's across the room. Wearing worn jeans, a flannel shirt with the sleeves rolled to his elbows, and ancient boots, he looked like the man she'd loved beyond reason. Add in the unshaven jaw and dirty-blond hair gathered in a high knot, he looked more like he was in the middle of a magazine spread than an actual workingman—gorgeous. Cameron had always been gorgeous. And hurt. Her pulse rate quickened when she saw the bloody rag wrapped around his left hand.

She rushed across the room. "What happened?"

"Not used to the big circular yet. Good thing I was only cleaning the blade and not actually running it."

Carefully, she removed the rag. Lord, why couldn't they have something clean out at the mill? Whenever someone out there got hurt, they always came to the clinic with the wound covered or wrapped in something filthy. And she knew with absolute certainty that there was a perfectly nice first aid kit in the office. She'd put it there herself and instructed Camille to keep it stocked.

"You always looked good in blue."

She glanced up at him from her kneeling position in front of his chair. He offered her a small smile, almost apologetic.

Knowing no one looked good in scrubs, be they blue or covered in rainbows, she smiled wryly and returned her focus to his hand. He'd nicked his thumb pretty good, and it would require at least a few stitches.

"You'll live." She rose and looked around. "Though I think we need to ask Mary and Mr. Evans if they're okay with you seeing the doctor first since the wound is still bleeding."

"Of course," Mary Solomon replied at the same time as Mr. Evans took it one step further with his, "Best get that young man of yours stitched up as soon as possible."

"Thank you both. I'll be right back." Skye suspected her cheeks had gone bright red as hot as they felt when she escaped out the back to find something clean to wrap Cameron's hand in until her daddy was finished with his current patient. It was a woman who came in regularly to complain about new aches and pains, though her only real issue was loneliness.

Skye put a temporary dressing on Cam's finger then showed him into her daddy's office when the coast was clear.

Her daddy looked at them over the rim of his glasses as they entered. "Cameron."

"Hello, Doc."

"Cameron cut his finger on a saw at the mill," Skye explained before greetings escalated into something she didn't want to hear. She knew very well her daddy still held a grudge against Cameron.

"The big circular? Sends me plenty of business, that one. Have a seat." Her daddy examined the wound, unknowingly agreeing with Skye assessment of stitches. "When was your last tetanus shot?"

"Last time you gave me one."

"That long, huh? We'll throw in one of those as well, then."

Skye was certain it had never taken so long to stitch up a cut and administer a tetanus shot before. Any moment, she expected someone to say the wrong thing and set her daddy off, giving Cameron the tongue-lashing he'd waited six years to deliver.

"I'm awful sorry about your daddy," she heard him say to Cameron instead.

"Thanks." Cameron cleared his throat. "Would he...I mean, can you say...did he suffer?"

"No, son, he didn't. A stroke is a contradiction, as it shows as much mercy to the patient due to its quickness as it shows none to those left behind unexpectedly."

Cameron nodded. "Thanks for telling me."

Her daddy finished up, sticking, stitching, and bandaging. "Keep it dry and preferably away from saws of any kind. The stitches will dissolve on their own. Did you drive here on your own?"

Cameron nodded.

"You've lost a bit of blood, so I'd like it if you took a seat out back and drank some juice before driving off. Skye will show you."

"Thanks, Doc."

Her daddy smiled unexpectedly. "Good seeing you again, Cameron, though next time we'll just run into each other on the street, all right?"

"Yes, sir."

Skye went with Cameron back to the waiting room and got him a bottle of orange juice before showing Mr. Evans in. She'd already taken care of his blood work, but he needed a pep talk from the doctor—he had a hard time staying away from sweets. Her daddy did pep talks much better than she did.

When Mr. Evans and Mary had been seen to, Skye returned to the waiting room. Cameron was staring out the window while absently toying with the edge of the bandage. He looked absolutely miserable. Lost. Everything in her screamed to go to him, but she wasn't sure it was wise given their history. If she went to him, comforted him, and gave him everything she had, he could easily take it all away again. Burned once, twice shy. She wasn't sure she could survive being stripped bare again.

* * * *

His finger—hell, half his hand—was numb. He wished the rest of him were as blissfully unaware of the pain gnawing through him. He'd been careless earlier, lost in thought at the big saw. If only he had been able to stop the bleeding, he'd have been able to avoid going to the clinic. Doc Jones had been surprisingly nice considering Cameron had run out on his daughter, though. The doc had always been nice, Mrs. Jones too. Cameron smiled to himself. Maybe it was because he had no memories of his own momma, nor had any real kind of relationship with his daddy's later wives, but he'd always seen Mrs. Jones as the essence of what a real mother was like. A kind smile, a tin full of freshly baked cookies, a shoulder to cry on, always ready with an answer to every question.

He finished his juice and looked around for a trashcan. Then saw Skye in the door, pity radiating from her.

Cameron stood up abruptly. "What?"

"Nothing," she said. Her voice was calm, but there was a storm raging in her eyes. "I was just coming to check up on you. Any wooziness or pain?"

"No, Nurse Jones. Nothing. I'm fine, good to go. Thanks." He walked out, aware that he had sneered as badly as Straw did when he'd mentioned her title.

"Cam."

"What?"

She grabbed his arm, and he stopped but didn't turn around to face her. "I don't know what that was about, and I certainly don't want to hold a busy man such as yourself up. But that finger is going to hurt later, so take these. The dose is on the package."

Cameron accepted the small container of painkillers and watched Skye stalk down the hall, her rigid back telling him what he already knew. He'd pissed her off, possibly on purpose because it was better to have her mad at him than pitying him. Part of him felt bad, but he didn't feel bad enough to go apologize. He didn't need anyone's pity, least of all hers. What reason did she have to pity him anyway?

He walked out the way he had come in. There were new patients in the waiting room, and he nodded to them as he went through. He hadn't even closed the door behind him before he heard the first whisper. It made him think about how he'd once told his daddy how much he hated living in Maeville because people did nothing but gossip about each other. His daddy had replied that if he stopped doing dumb things, people would stop gossiping. Now he wondered what dumb thing he'd done lately other than return home.

One last look toward the clinic revealed Skye looking out through the window. She quickly disappeared from view when she realized she'd been spotted. With a sigh he put on the jacket he had left in the truck and started the drive home.

That night he got out of helping Hunter and Straw move back into the house because of his damaged digit. Instead he cooked one of the few things that made up his limited cooking repertoire. Burgers. While cooking and listening to Straw bitch as he was carrying in his stuff, Cameron thought of all the headaches ahead.

They had never been able to agree on chores as kids, and back then they'd had their daddy to referee, plus they'd actually been friends—brothers. Agreeing on who cooked, cleaned, did laundry now was going to be World War III, full steam ahead with dirty bombs and no Geneva Convention.

"You got more stuff coming from Nashville?" Reid asked, stopping in the door. He'd selflessly offered to help move boxes from Hunter's cabin up river and from Straw's apartment downtown since he always traveled light, never owning more than what he could have on his sailboat.

"Nope." Failures traveled light, he'd discovered. All his worldly possessions fit into his truck.

Reid crossed his arms and leaned against the doorframe. "Won't your fans be disappointed you're canceling concerts or whatever?"

"I had nothing planned," Cameron replied, turning to reach for plates and stubbed his thumb for the thirtieth time. Swore.

"Gotcha."

Cameron took a deep breath when Reid wandered off. Even before he had left for Nashville, he'd been dreaming of the day when he could come and tell everyone about his music career, about his success, about his dreams coming true despite what everyone had thought. Show them all how wrong they had been about him. That had been pride mixed with the kind of confidence only the young and naïve were able to pull off. These days only pride remained, and all it did was keep him from slipping down the slippery slope and into the mess that the truth about his time in Nashville was.

Dinner was eaten in awkward silence. Hunter had lost some of his enthusiasm for carrying out their daddy's last wishes when he'd realized he would have to give up his privacy and move in with the rest of them, and Cameron thought he might have figured out Straw. The kid didn't sneer and complain because he disliked something. It was just his unfortunate—and highly annoying—way of communicating. Once a brat, always a brat.

When the meal was over, Cameron found himself alone in the kitchen again. He could hear the TV being turned on in the living room, and loud music started blaring from upstairs. He looked around at the mess his cooking had produced and swore out loud. Hell if he was cooking *and* cleaning up. He wasn't anyone's maid.

Instead, he went outside. Being back in Maeville was a walk down memory lane, memories he hadn't given any thought for years popping unbidden into his head. Pretty much all of them featured his brothers, his daddy, or Skye. It was a shame he'd been so consumed by his dreams that he'd forgotten to treasure them while they were happening.

Hunter came down the porch steps. "I'm already regretting this."

Cameron looked up at the window to Straw's room. It was a wonder the neighbors hadn't been over to complain about the loud music. "Why the hell is he so angry?"

Pulling on his jacket, Hunter sighed. "I don't even know where to start. I think he feels screwed over by the world in general and his family in particular. Or maybe the other way around. Charlene was never momma of the year. Daddy tried to understand him, but I'm not sure Straw actually wants to be understood. He resents me for trying to help because he thinks I'm lecturing, and he resents you and Reid for doing what he wanted to—getting out of town."

"No one stopped him from leaving."

"No one but himself. That's another person Straw resents. You and Reid chased your dreams out of town. Maybe there isn't any room left for dreams inside a man that filled with anger." Hunter stuck his hands into his pockets. "I'm going out for a beer. I really hope the kitchen is cleaned up when I get back."

Cameron snorted. "I cooked. Someone else can clean."

Hunter walked down the pathway. "You made the mess."

"Fucking brothers," Cameron muttered to himself as he watched Hunter disappear. There was no way he was cleaning up the kitchen.

\* \* \* \*

"Your daddy said Cameron was at the clinic today."

Skye took the biscuits out of the oven and glanced at her momma. "Yes, he was."

"You should have invited him over for dinner. Heaven knows when the boy last had a nice, home-cooked meal."

"You'll have to invite him yourself if you want him to come to dinner." Skye didn't take offense by her momma's words. She was the most forgiving person in the world, so although she'd been ready to go mama bear on Cameron when he had left, she'd long ago forgiven him. Her daddy, on the other hand, wasn't usually so quick to forgive, although he'd been pleasant enough to Cameron earlier at the clinic. And as for Skye, she was still undecided. It was difficult to hold a grudge against someone she'd discovered she wasn't over yet.

"I just might, but only if you get used to the idea."

Skye just smiled and put the biscuits on the table. She treasured joining her parents for dinner once or twice a week, but she wasn't sure if she would like to be there if Cameron was asked over.

Shortly after her daddy had said grace, he turned the conversation to Cameron again. "I was surprised to see he'd been working at the sawmill. Seeing him come into my office was like seeing him years ago. You don't work at that mill and not get a scrape once in a while."

"It sure is nice of him to stay and help when he's got a big career over in Nashville," her momma commented. "Don't you think, Skye?"

"Yes, Momma."

"I wonder why, though." Passing the beans around, her momma's gaze landed on Skye. "Do you know?"

"No, I haven't talked to Cam about it."

"You didn't talk to him after I'd stitched him up?" her daddy asked.

Skye prayed for strength. Being interrogated by her parents about Cameron was supposed to be a thing of the past. She'd thought it over and done with six years ago when she had finally gotten them to understand that she had no idea why Cameron had left without telling her why, asking her to come, or propose to her like they, as well as the rest of the town, had expected. "No, Daddy. He wasn't in the best of moods after. Maybe the local was wearing off."

"Well, it's nice that he's back even if the occasion is a sad one. Reid, too. I wonder how they're all getting along."

Skye tuned out the conversation when she realized she'd shredded the napkin in her lap. Cameron had been an ass earlier, and the more she thought about the dig he'd taken at her profession, the angrier she got. How dared he assume that he was better than her? She was the one with a successful, well-balanced life, the achieved goals, the dream that had come true. Not him. Skye normally did her best to let go of anger, finding it a waste of time to go around being mad at things she couldn't do anything about anyway. Cameron, of course, was the exception like he was in so many other ways. Damn him and the day he'd rolled back into town.

Since she was so preoccupied and not in the mood to listen to her parents discuss the Madigans all night, she left early and was weak enough to let Camille lure her down to the local bar for a beer.

Camille was already there when Skye came in, as was Hunter, Sam who worked at the sawmill, his wife Wendy, and some guy Skye couldn't remember the name of. Part of the usual gang, but this time when she saw Camille and Hunter together, Skye couldn't help but study them in a different light.

She went over to the table they all occupied. "Hey, y'all."

Camille scooted over and made room for her, and soon the relaxed atmosphere with absolutely no mentions of Cameron gave her the peace she'd been in need of since seeing him earlier. It didn't last, however. Few things ever did.

"So, boss. How long are your brothers in town for?" Camille asked Hunter.

Hunter sent her an unimpressed look. "Quit calling me boss."

"But you are my boss."

"All right. I'll just call you *employee* then."

Skye snickered and found her curiosity peaked. "Terms of endearment aside, how long are they staying?"

Hunter leaned back in his seat and smiled lazily. Skye supposed that if she hadn't thought of him as family for so long, the smile would be quite lethal. Cameron's version of it certainly was.

"I could tell you, but I'm afraid you might keel over in shock if I do."

"I'm a nurse," Skye reminded him. "I can handle a small medical emergency."

Putting his beer down, Hunter leaned in after checking that the rest of the party was engaged in conversation at the other end of the table. "I'd appreciate it if you didn't spread this all over town yet. No need to add unnecessary pressure. Daddy's will stipulated that we all have to live and work together for a year to receive the inheritance."

"You're kidding," Camille exclaimed, eyes wide.

"Nope."

"And what if someone leaves? Do the others share or what?"

All traces of the smile disappeared from Hunter's face. "If someone leaves…well, if any of them leaves…for some reason Daddy was certain that I wouldn't…but if one leaves, the others get nothing. And I inherit everything on my own."

"That's putting a lot on your shoulders," Camille pointed out. "Do you want them to leave?"

"No, I want them to stay. I'm just not sure they believe I'm being sincere. And I'm not sure if what Daddy wanted is even possible without starting a war on Madigan Avenue."

Skye listened in silence, wondering if she was the only one who understood the web of complications Cameron was busy tangling himself in. She didn't know for sure if someone else might have discovered the secret he apparently thought he could keep forever.

# Chapter Six

"Why should I go grocery shopping again? None of you have pitched in yet. I'm not your goddamn momma!" Hunter slammed the refrigerator door. "And someone better clean this shit up."

"It's Cam's mess," Straw said, arms crossed stubbornly across his chest.

"I cooked, so someone else should clean. And I'm not cooking again today."

"Strawberry can do it," Reid suggested helpfully. "He got out of too many chores as a kid because he was such a baby."

"Fuck you." Straw stomped out, loud music signaling the moment he reached his room.

"And apparently he's still a baby." Cam sighed, picking the lesser evil. "I'll go out for groceries. But that gets me out of cleaning and cooking."

Hunter rolled his eyes. "I'll clean this up. Reid, you go shut up Straw and that horrible noise he calls music."

"Yeah, it sure ain't Cameron Madigan's greatest hits." Reid looked up at the ceiling. "Fucking Strawberry."

Cameron hurried out. Though Straw's taste in music left a lot to be desired, it would have been a lot worse if he'd been blaring Cameron's album. Thank heavens for crappy little brothers.

He drove to the grocery store and took exactly three steps inside before he realized he hadn't picked the lesser evil, after all. Mrs. Schwartz, his old English teacher, zeroed in on him and came limping over on that right leg that was inches shorter than the left one. He'd never understood why she could enjoy teaching as much as she did—or had, as she'd be retired now—when kids were so cruel to anyone on the interesting side of normal.

"Cameron Madigan, I do declare. I heard you came back for your daddy's funeral. Bless his heart. I'm so sorry for your loss, but it sure is good to see your handsome face. How are you?"

"I'm good, Mrs. Schwartz. You look mighty pretty in that hat." Truth was it looked like a fruit bowl, reminding Cameron how hungry he was and that he was here for dinner ingredients. "Life must be agreeing with you."

"Listen to you, you charmer. I can't complain." She tucked her arm under his. "I keep scouring the newspapers and magazines for news about Maeville's biggest star, but they'd rather write about tragedies and stupid people running their cars into telephone poles and whatnot. Nashville still keeping you happy?"

"Actually, Mrs. Schwartz, I've decided to come home, at least for the time being. We decided to stick together and keep the sawmill running." Lying was a dangerous habit, Cameron reminded himself, though he didn't know what else he could say.

"Dear boy, that's the most selfish act I've ever heard of. Giving up your career to come home and help your family." She reached up and patted his cheek. "Your daddy would have been proud of you."

Cameron felt like the biggest fraud, but he managed a grimace. "It was wonderful to see you again, but I best be going, or I'll have three starving brothers on my hands."

"Oh, well. We can't have that, can we? You take care of yourself, Cameron Madigan."

"You too, ma'am."

Allowing himself a sigh of relief, he grabbed a cart and went hunting for food before he ran into someone else who thought he looked like he had time to stop and chat. He had no idea if his brothers still had the same likes and dislikes, but they'd better eat what he got or they could get their own damn groceries.

Thirty minutes later the cart was full and he had been stopped four times. And to think that he'd once dreamed of having fans and getting recognized on the street. Clearly, he'd been insane.

Reid cooked dinner that night, complaining loudly that Cameron hadn't bought any fish.

"You're not on a damn boat now," Straw was kind enough to inform Reid, who took time from chopping onions to flip his younger brother the finger. Straw sported a new black eye, and Reid had a cut lip. Cameron figured it was from the music discussion and that Reid had won since everyone's eardrums were safe for now.

"We should make some kind of schedule for the chores," Hunter said. "Fighting it out every day is bound to get old soon."

"Fighting works for me," Straw disagreed. He was so predictable.

"Odds are, Strawberry, that you're outnumbered," Hunter pointed out.

"Odds are, asshole, that I'll fight you even if you do make a schedule. My name is Julian."

"His name is Julian," Reid parroted like he had since he was old enough to see how much it annoyed Straw.

"Fuck this. I'm going out." Hunter rose and left the kitchen.

Five minutes later, when Straw and Reid were fighting again and knocking over everything in their path, Cameron got up, too. He'd get a sandwich later. Maybe later all of them would also start like behaving like adults.

He went down to the river and, too restless to settle, followed it downstream for a while. He ended up down at the old, closed bridge where he'd run into Skye that first night back in town. He hadn't been thinking of her specifically, but like a mirage, she was there again. Hugging a book to her chest, she was staring straight ahead with something close to a smile, but not quite, on her face. Twilight had taken hold of the forest, and she looked like she might disappear into it with her black hair and dark green jacket. A wood nymph—he'd often compared her to one in the past.

She had an ethereal beauty that knocked the breath out of any man with a pulse. She'd been his once, and he had been stupid enough to throw her away. Like she could hear his thoughts, she turned her head. The maybe-smile disappeared completely when she saw him.

* * * *

She'd been thinking about him, though she didn't realize it until he materialized out of thin air. If she hadn't known him, she'd have been afraid. There wasn't always peace in Cameron's face, and when the smile was far away, he got the look of someone who daddies warned their daughters about. Not that the lethal smile he possessed was any less dangerous, but there was charm in it that few could resist. Skye had certainly never been able to, though to be fair, she'd never been able to resist the brooding side of him either, the one with all the faraway dreams.

It was getting dark, and she had been on her way home when a wisp of fog or mist between the trees across the river had caught her attention and pulled her into a daydream about a mystical forest that even now her fingers were itching to write down as song lyrics. She got her best material from tales spun in her own mind.

"Hey, sugar."

"Six years is a long time, Cam, but not quite long enough for me to forget that when you say *hey, sugar* in that particular tone, it's because you want something. And to be honest, I don't think I have anything left I want to give," she told him, her tone resigned. It was raw honesty, and perhaps more than she'd intended to say to him. Running into him just as twilight started to give way to the dark by the river was already a bad habit. With the day's last shadows slinking around them, she felt too vulnerable to be around him, especially in a place where they had so many shared memories.

"I just want to apologize for yesterday at the clinic. The way you looked at me…well, it hit a nerve. And I'm sorry."

Skye started up the bank, but was too curious to keep going. She stopped and studied him. "And what way did I look at you that was so offensive?"

"Not offensive...just...you looked like you were pitying me."

It had been, and she wasn't surprised it had struck a cord. But she *was* surprised he was admitting it. "What reason do I have to pity you?"

"Beats me." But he didn't look at her.

"In that case you must have been mistaken."

"Maybe." He came closer. "Isn't it a bit cold to sit and read down here?"

"I wasn't reading. I still come down here to write."

"That desk drawer must be overflowing by now." He shook his head. "Why the hell are you wasting your time in Maeville being a nurse when you could be writing music for the best singers out there?"

"Such as yourself?" Skye asked sweetly.

"No. Fuck. But you have a talent, one that very few possess."

"I know very well what my talents are, Cam, and it's none of your business what I do with them. You just worry about your own."

Cameron laughed humorlessly. "Yeah, I'll do that."

"And for someone who came to apologize for sneering at my profession, sneering at it again isn't the way to go. Consider it your tip of the day." Skye started the trek back to the road, hearing Cameron behind her. She really hated how much he was still able to get to her.

"You used to have dreams," he called out after her. "Have you forgotten them?"

"You know nothing, Cameron." Absolutely nothing. She was steamed by the time she reached the lit road, but luckily she couldn't hear him behind her anymore. The nerve of him. Not only had he ruined her peaceful mood, he'd also chased away the song in her head just waiting to be written down. And he talked about wasting talents.

Skye headed home to her beloved cabin, determined to get back the song with the help of a glass of wine and some breathing exercises. Cameron Madigan wasn't stealing her lyrics.

Walking up the path to her home, she jumped and swallowed a scream when a figure stepped out from the shadows. Her heart beat painfully in her chest until she realized that Cameron had beaten her there, probably by going by the river instead of by the road.

"Why don't you just shoot me next time? It'll be quicker." She fought to regain control of her breathing. "What the hell are you doing here?"

"I don't know." He had his hands in his pockets, and his face was covered in shadows from the porch light that turned on automatically. "Yes, I do. I keep fucking up, and I really don't mean to. I'm sorry."

"Until next time I'm sure." Skye sighed. "Look, it doesn't matter what you think of my job, my decisions, my life. We're not friends, and I don't need your approval. I understand that you're struggling right now, but it's got nothing to do with me."

He hesitated. "We could be friends."

"Could we really?"

"I think so."

"You'll excuse me if I have trouble seeing it. And why now?" She found her keys in her pocket. "You think about that for a while. Goodnight, Cam."

She felt a little bad about going in and leaving him out there. He really was struggling, but no matter how much part of her wanted to comfort him and make it all better, she didn't need his issues dumped in her lap after he'd ignored her for years. Actions had consequences, and if Cameron hadn't learned that in Nashville, he would just have to learn it now.

* * * *

A restless night meant that Cameron got an early start the following morning. Grabbing breakfast and coffee on the run before anyone else got up, ignoring the still messy kitchen, he headed straight to the mill. In the days he had been back, he'd only just fallen back into old routines. He hadn't taken time to check out the whole place yet.

The morning mist lay heavy over the quiet mill. Cameron already knew his ever-industrious daddy had expanded the operation in the past six years, especially with the row of furniture workshops that Hunter apparently had been managing even before…well, before. It was late in the year, so seasonal workers had already been hired to do the Christmas tree part, cutting down and selling them on the town green. They'd replant in the spring. In the past they'd also opened part of the forest for people who wanted to cut down their own tree for the holidays, using part of the lot for Christmas markets the last four Sundays before Christmas. He wondered if that was a tradition they would be carrying on and who would be deciding it.

The regular mill business was what he was most familiar with. They had all started out with the easy stuff like handling byproducts, and then they had rotated around until they found out where they belonged. Hunter had been a logger when Cameron left, but now he'd moved onto making furniture. Reid had always been most comfortable around the customers, and he'd fallen back into that role naturally. Straw didn't seem to have moved beyond byproducts and the debarking machine. For himself, Cameron was most comfortable with the big saws, but he wondered if maybe it wasn't time for another rotation to see if there was something else he might enjoy now that he'd lost the resentment against anything sawmill related. It would also give his sore thumb a break.

"I thought that was you. You're here early." Camille strolled over to where Cameron had been lost in thought. She was bundled up as if she was expecting a snowstorm.

He'd always liked her, although for a long time he'd struggled to understand her complete loyalty to his daddy.

"Morning. Do we pay you enough to get here this early?"

She smiled and shrugged. "Just thought I'd come in and clean the office."

"We pay you to do *that*?"

"You don't pay anyone else to do it, but that's okay. I don't mind."

"You do payroll, right?"

She nodded.

"Give yourself a raise. You deserve it."

Camille laughed. "Maybe I'm being a bad friend to someone I care about a lot, but it's nice to have you home, Cameron. I'll talk to Hunter about the raise sometime."

He got slightly offended before he realized that no one knew the content of his daddy's will. Maybe they assumed he'd left the mill to his sons, maybe they assumed he'd left it to the perfect son, Hunter, and that he and his brothers were just staying to help out. They hadn't talked about keeping the will a secret, most likely because agreeing on something as simple as whose turn it was to take out the trash was like pulling teeth.

Camille wasn't just anyone, however. She'd been the backbone of the business long before Cameron left town, the one who made sure things ran smoothly. His daddy had been damn lucky to find someone as loyal, competent, and sweet as Camille Bradford, and Cameron was glad that the old man had known to appreciate it. The sum set aside for her in the will showed that.

"Did anyone tell you what was in the will?" Cameron asked.

"You mean that your daddy left me fifty thousand dollars?"

He hadn't known the amount, but whatever his daddy wanted her to have was fine with him. "Besides that."

She gnawed on her lip. "Kinda?"

"It's not a trick question. I just...well, I thought it was fair you knew. You kind of run this place, although I'm sure Hunter—and Daddy—thought they did. He left everything, except the money for you, to all of us on the condition that we stay at the house and work here for a year. If just one of us ups and leaves, it all goes to Hunter."

"Hunter might have mentioned something about that," she admitted. "He said not to tell anyone, though. No need to add more pressure. Are you...no, never mind."

"Am I what?"

She pulled at the strings on her knitted hat with earflaps. "No, it's rude."

"I won't take offense, I promise."

"Okay." She hesitated. "Are you staying just for the inheritance? Bailing after a year?"

Camille looked like an angel with her sky blue eyes, long blonde hair, and impish dimples. Her heart was the size of a small country, and her mind worked in mysterious ways, often saying the last thing he expected. Out of everyone, he really should have expected to get that question from her. What was worse, he felt like being honest with her. All this honesty was bound to make the truth slip out sooner or later. He'd be the laughed out of town.

"I don't know. I didn't think I'd want to stay, but now that I'm here, I don't see any reason to leave again."

"What about your career?"

He spotted Hunter and Reid walking toward them and smiled sadly at Camille. "Sometimes the dream is the best part."

Happy about the interruption, he said nothing when Reid started peppering Camille with questions about the preparations for the Christmas markets. Hunter glared at him before turning around, walking back the way he'd just come.

"I'll see you guys later," Cameron said and walked off in the opposite direction. He had no idea what he'd done to offend Hunter, nor did he have the slightest clue why he'd just been more honest with Camille than he'd been with anyone in years. He needed to get to work and use his muscles until they burned every thought right out of his mind. That was his plan, and he was sticking to it come hell or high water.

# Chapter Seven

Every once in a while, Skye took the day off and drove the hundred miles to Rocky Mount. She let people think she was doing it to unwind, to shop for more shoes she didn't need, or whatever else they conjured up. It made no difference to her since no one would ever come even close to guessing the truth.

The truth was that she was meeting André.

If she hadn't still been on the rebound when they'd first met, she might have fallen for him. He was funny, smart, sexy as sin. He was also a good friend, and since their first meeting a little over five years ago, he had met the love of his life and married her. They had a baby on the way. And for almost a decade, he'd been providing some of Nashville's biggest stars with one hit after the other. For half that, he'd had a mysterious writing partner by the name of Blue Skies.

About six months after Cameron's departure, Skye had pulled herself enough together to say *screw him* and work on those dreams they'd used to share. So he had ridden off into the sunset to become a star without her. That didn't mean she couldn't work hard to make her own dreams come true. She'd never wanted to be a star. The spotlight held no allure for her, but music did. Weaving music and words together was what she'd always wanted. So she did just that. She poured her heartbreak—*thanks, Cam*—into songs and sent them to every music-related address in Nashville she could find. That's how André had discovered her, and they'd built up a successful partnership since. He was more than happy to use his own face and let her stay in the background. At first, she hadn't wanted to admit how she didn't think she could do it without Cameron. Later on, when her songwriting career had taken off, she'd discovered she liked the anonymity of hiding behind a penname and André. That way, she could have the best of both worlds—her dream and her daily life.

"Skye. As pretty as ever," he greeted her when she entered their usual coffee house.

"André. As predictable as ever."

He laughed as she sat down in front of the white chocolate espresso he'd already ordered for her. "We need to come up with a new opening routine, don't we?"

"Maybe next year." Skye sipped her espresso. "How have you been? How's Tracy?"

"Tracy is great, enjoying pregnancy and making me run around like a lunatic trying to keep up with all her cravings. I thought they were just a myth, but she's going all out with the weird stuff. Last night it was sardines and bananas."

Skye wrinkled her nose in sympathy.

"What about you?" André asked, sipping his own coffee. "Word has it Cameron Madigan left Nashville and went back home."

Narrowing her eyes over the rim of her cup, she wondered how much to tell him. André had pieced together a surprisingly large part of her story after she'd first mentioned Cameron's name to him. Since then he'd kept her up to date with news from Nashville whether she'd wanted to hear it or not. "Word has it? You're keeping tabs on him just so you can torture me."

André shrugged, an amused look on his face. "Just doing you a favor, darlin'."

"Gee, thanks. I hate to disappoint you, but I'm fine even though Cameron is back in Maeville." She put down her cup. "His daddy died recently."

"That's rough."

"Life's rough. That's why country's so popular."

They discussed what they'd been working on individually and together lately. The face-to-face meetings weren't strictly necessary other than from a social viewpoint, as they'd long ago mastered the art of writing songs together via e-mail attachments. But touching base was nice, so André flew into Rocky Mount once in a while, and Skye made the drive. It wasn't Nashville, it wasn't Maeville; it was a nice compromise.

It was a profitable venture they had going because they complimented each other so well. Skye could twist emotions into the lyrics like few others in the business, and André knew just how to make the melody memorable. If she'd wanted to, Skye could become as big of a star as André was in the music world. She hadn't been tempted, not even when she discovered that she could have gotten the last word in with Cameron. It just wasn't who she was.

Driving home with big news about all the stars who were queuing up for their songs and a new pair of shoes—alibi or not, a girl needed new shoes, especially when she had herself a lucrative second job that no one but her best friend and her parents knew even the slightest bit about back home—Skye was in a great mood. She hummed along to the radio, grinning when one of her own songs came on sung by one of Nashville's heavy-weighters.

Just outside Maeville, she spotted a truck with the Madigan Sawmill's logo on the side pulled onto the shoulder of the road. Slowing down, she spotted someone sitting on the ground, so she pulled over, too.

It was Julian. Seeming not to notice the cold, he sat on the ground wearing only a t-shirt, stained jeans, and boots. He was smoking and looked up almost lazily when she neared him.

"Hi, Julian. Are you okay?"

"Just dandy." He looked around. "What are you doing out here?"

"I was just about to ask you the same thing. I'm driving back from Rocky Mount."

"Huh." Nodding, he focused on his cigarette. Skye was worried he'd been in some kind of accident. He looked confused, out of it almost.

"Julian, what are you doing out here?"

"I like the way you say that. My name. Not Straw or Strawberry. Not kid." He smiled at her and leaned his head back against the truck. "What are you doing out here?"

It was the smile that tipped her off. He wasn't hurt; he was either drunk or high.

She kneeled down in front of him. "Why don't I drive you home?"

"I got a truck."

"I know, but I'd like you to keep me company."

He staggered to his feet, waving away her offered hand. "Always knew you'd realize Cam's a pussy."

Skye rolled her eyes and guided Julian back to her car. One part of her wanted to slap him until he woke up and realized he was wasting his life. Another part of her wanted to cry for the young, broken man who was clearly so lost.

* * * *

Cameron had just gotten out of the shower after a long day at the mill when he heard the doorbell. Not really in the mood for company—mainly because company meant nosy, gossiping people—he ignored it and hoped someone else would answer. Hunter and Reid were around somewhere…maybe. When the bell rang out again, he looked out the window. There was a car parked out on the street. Swearing under his breath, he went downstairs while pulling his wet hair back. Wrenching the door open, ready to tell whoever was outside to get lost, he was surprised to see Skye propping up a grinning Straw.

"A little help here please?" she said curtly.

"Is he sick?"

"More like drunk or high."

"Then dump him anywhere. I'm not his momma."

Blowing out an exasperated breath, she did just that. Straw immediately curled up and closed his eyes.

"I found him outside of town next to one of the mills' trucks. I thought he was hurt."

"He's gonna be plenty hurt tomorrow." Cameron glanced at Straw when be started to snore. "Thanks for bringing him home. I'm not sure what to do with him, but at least he's safer on the porch than on the side of the road."

"You could haul him inside, you know. Dump him into bed. Make sure he doesn't choke on his own vomit when the buzz wears off."

"I could," Cameron agreed, folding his arms across his chest and enjoying the look of her. She'd always looked spectacular when she was a little riled up or offended about something. Right now it was at him, and possibly his hopeless brother, but it didn't matter. He'd always preferred storm clouds to the fluffy white ones on a summer day.

"But you won't," she stated flatly.

"Probably not. If he's drinking by the side of the road, sleeping it off on a safe porch is more than what he deserves. Does he do this a lot?"

Skye hesitated. Did her loyalty really lie with Straw rather than him these days?

"I've never found him by the side of the road before, but I have seen him wasted around town. Usually it's in the company of those so-called friends of his. They fancy themselves a motorcycle gang or something. They make a bit of trouble sometimes, fighting, breaking things. Hunter thinks one of them is selling drugs."

"That's just great. Any excuse to waste his life for our Strawberry."

"He hates being called that."

"Yeah? Maybe when he grows up, we'll call him something else."

Skye's eyes shot fire. "He hasn't had an easy life."

"Last time I checked, I was the only orphan of the Madigan Family. So his momma's hopeless, but she isn't dead."

"Poor Cameron. Maybe it's time you checked again, though. And don't forget you've got a truck sitting on the side of the road."

There was no mistaking the angry stride down through the front yard, nor the slam of the car door. He stared after her until the car disappeared from sight. So he'd laid on the self-pity a little thick. But it was true. Although their mommas wouldn't be winning any parenting awards, his brothers still had one parent left somewhere. He froze. Or had he missed something monumental? Shit.

Leaving Straw where he was—he'd haul him inside later—Cameron headed for the living room and the old family bible that had resided in the house since his great-great-great-granddaddy had built it hundred and fifty years earlier. Cameron had been sixteen before his daddy had allowed him to even touch the heirloom. Now he took it reverently down from the shelf and looked in the back where all births, marriages, and deaths in direct line after William Madigan were recorded.

The first thing he noticed was that his daddy's death hadn't been entered. Perhaps that was his job as the oldest son. Perhaps it was Hunter's as the favorite. The last death entry should have been Cameron's own momma. She'd died giving him life. But it wasn't the last entry. Estelle Madigan had passed away a little over a year ago.

Cameron didn't have a lot of memories of Hunter's momma. She and his daddy had divorced when he was about four years old, and although he remembered her all but begging his daddy to let him go with Hunter when he visited her up in the city, he'd never been allowed. Hunter had lived with her only in brief periods, never developing a taste for the city and preferring the quiet life in Maeville.

And now she was gone. Cameron knew he had no reason to feel bad; he hadn't known at the time as he'd had no contact with anyone from his family a year ago, but he still felt a twinge of guilt he hadn't been there for Hunter. Not because they were particularly good at being there for each other now, but he hated the thought and the realization that he actually knew very little about the brothers he was now living with again.

Stopping only to pick up his jacket and to haul Straw into the house, he left the house that started to feel claustrophobic as soon as he began analyzing his own worth as a brother. He'd failed at many things over the years. Failed in epic ways and failed in small ways. And he was only now starting to understand that he'd failed in every way that was truly important. He'd failed with Skye, he'd failed with his daddy, and he'd failed with his brothers. Those failures had been eclipsed completely by the one failure that had seemed so much more important.

His failed career.

His ruined dream.

He hadn't been aware of where he was going, but when he finally stopped, he wasn't surprised. He was standing in front of his daddy's grave. There was a headstone on it now, stating the bare facts about a man who'd been so much more than the days he'd entered and left the world. Faded flowers, as well as fresh ones, covered the grave. The stone was only one among many in the large, fenced family plot. The Madigans of yesterday.

"You were right," Cameron told his daddy's headstone and took a deep breath which came out on a wobbly exhale. He'd never said the words out loud before, never admitted his defeat. It sliced his insides to ribbons. "Damn you! You said I'd never amount to anything in the music business, and you were right."

Cameron started pacing in front of the plot. "And you knew me. You fucking knew me. Telling me I'd fail was the one thing that would make me more determined than ever to go and prove you wrong. If you knew I'd fail so miserably, why the hell didn't you just tell me straight? You just *had* to sneer, taunt, and belittle me, making sure I went all out and failed as spectacularly as possibly. You bastard."

Stopping in front of his momma's headstone, he wiped what were most certainly not tears from his eyes. "You know, Momma, whenever Daddy was being a bastard, I told myself that I was more like you than him. What the hell did I know, huh? I don't know what you were like. I just know that you left me, too. Maybe you were a bastard as well, making your marriage the perfect match. I don't fucking know, do I? I never got the chance to know. But I know something now. I'm as much of a bastard as my old man, and I really wish you'd been around so you could have changed both of us.

"Do either of you have any idea what it's like to walk onto a stage and face a near empty room? What it's like the first time you sacrifice yourself and your dream by taking a crappy job? When your record company and your manager stop taking your calls? Do you know exactly how much it hurts when you realize that your dream is in shreds at your feet, and that you can't possibly face your family because they'll laugh in your face and say *I told you so*, which just might break your heart completely?"

Cameron kicked at the low fence. "No, of course you don't know. You just left. You're no better than me, but I had to come back. You didn't even do that."

It was cold, and he was staring to feel it. Scrubbing his hands over his face, he laughed bitterly, feeling as crazy as he no doubt sounded, laughing in front of his daddy's fresh grave. "And the kicker? Do you know what it feels like to screw up your life completely and not realize it until months later? I had it all, didn't I? I had the woman of my dreams, I had a home, a steady job, a nice dream to keep me on my toes. And I tossed it all away by leaving. Took me blowing my dream to fathom what I'd done. And by then it was too late. It's all too late. Hunter hates us, Reid doesn't give a damn, Straw's so screwed up, and I'm...I'm..."

Empty. Crushed. Drowning.

Without looking back, he left. Talking to ghosts wasn't going to make him any less crazy, and what had the shadows of his past buried behind him done for him, anyway? Blamed him for leaving, then done the same. What the hell was he supposed to do about a dead dream, an inheritance with impossible conditions, messed up brothers, and the woman of his dreams who thought he was worth less than what she might scrape off her shoe? Ghosts weren't going to help him straighten out the mess that was his life. How could they when he couldn't?

When he got back home, he went in through the backdoor and successfully evaded the others. He could hear the TV on, smell someone cooking, but he wasn't in the mood for company. He ought to seek out Hunter and somehow find the words to express his sympathy. That it was for a loss that had occurred more than a year ago wasn't important. Cameron owed him the words. The sentiment. As soon as he found the right words.

He made it to his room without running into anyone, and from the drawer in his bedside table, he drew out the worn velvet box he'd carried with him like a talisman for six years. Many times he'd been tempted to sell it—he'd certainly been in need of the money often enough. But he'd never been able to part with it.

The ring he'd bought for Skye.

It wasn't a symbol of naïve illusions as much as it had been the last tie he'd had to his old life for a long time. Still was in some ways. Too many ways. Or not enough. He wasn't sure. With a sigh, he put the ring away again. He had a truck to pick up.

# Chapter Eight

Skye was walking toward her parents' house with a song bouncing around in her head. She would rather have stayed home and written it down, fussed with it until it was just right, then polished it some more, but her momma had invited her over for Sunday brunch.

"Good morning," she called out as she walked into the house she'd grown up in.

"In here, honey."

Skye took off her coat, and headed into the kitchen. "Hey, Momma."

"There's my pretty girl. Be a dear and take this to the table. Your daddy's been grumbling about food for the past hour."

Skye grinned. He'd yet to embrace the concept of brunch since her momma insisted it meant that they didn't need breakfast. Her daddy was a man who loved traditions and routines, which most definitely included breakfast.

"Morning, Daddy. Amy Wilde give birth yet?"

"No. I expect I'll get a call the moment we sit down to eat. A man could starve around here."

"Tell me, Doctor Jones, how long can a person stay alive without food?"

He smiled wryly and looked back at the newspaper he'd been reading.

"I hear you gave Julian Madigan a lift home the other day," her momma said when they'd sat down to eat. "I asked your daddy about it, but he didn't know anything."

Skye figured the instinctive need to protect and help Julian stemmed mainly from pity. He was a difficult man to like with all his thorns, but she was sure she'd genuinely like him if he gave her the chance.

"I suppose the polite thing would be to say that I gave him a lift, but the truth is that I found him drunk or high outside town and drove him home because I was worried he'd hurt himself. I tried pawning him off on Cam, but he told me to dump him on the front porch, and that he'd already gotten better than he deserved."

Her momma sighed. "Those poor Madigan boys."

"Those poor Madigan boys are grown men, Patty."

"I know, but they haven't had it easy."

"Or made it easy for themselves." Putting his newspaper aside, Skye's daddy reached for the coffee. "Let's not forget what Cameron did before leaving town."

"You can quit talking in code. That stopped working when I was about six," Skye reminded her parents.

"We're not," her momma assured her, pushing the plate of pancakes across the table. "Here, have some more. I talked to Sebastian yesterday. He can't come home for Thanksgiving, but he'll be here for Christmas he says."

"It's a shame about Thanksgiving. I haven't seen him since the Fourth of July." Skye frowned, thinking of her busy brother up in New York. She'd once considered studying medicine and following in her daddy and older brother's footsteps, but she was glad she'd chosen nursing instead. If she had been as busy as Sebastian, there would have been no time for songwriting.

"I was thinking we might invite the Madigan boys over."

Skye and her daddy both stared.

"What? They'll be alone, won't they?"

"I guess." Skye wished she had as big a heart as her momma. She didn't even take offence that her own mother wanted to invite the man who'd dumped her on her ass over for Thanksgiving dinner. It was just a weird thought, and she was sure the tension between the Madigan brothers would make it a difficult dinner to get through. If they accepted, that was, and she doubted that very much. At least not all of them.

"If you want, dear. Would you be comfortable with it, Skye?"

Trust her daddy to think of that. She smiled. "Yes, I'll be fine."

"Of course you will." Her momma topped off her orange juice. "Men think we need them, but we really don't."

At that, Skye grinned. "Right." If only it was true. Despite waves of red alert warnings running through her brain, her heart couldn't think of a lot it needed more than Cameron Madigan.

By the end of brunch, Skye had somehow been roped into going with her momma to the Madigan house. She wasn't entirely sure how it had happened, but figured she could at least check how Julian was doing.

"It's such a beautiful house," her momma commented as they strolled down Madigan Avenue and the big, white house came into view.

"Yes, it is."

"Honey, are you sure you don't mind me inviting them? Inviting Cameron? I know it's a little unconventional, and the last thing I want is for you to be uncomfortable, but I just thought of how I'd like for someone in New York to do a little something special for my boy. And the Madigans don't have anyone. Heaven knows Reid and Julian's mommas are too busy gallivanting around to check up on their sons."

"I think it's very sweet of you to think of them. I'll be comfortable enough. Six years is a long time." Just not enough to get over the only man she'd ever really loved.

Satisfied with Skye's answer, her momma smiled and marched up to the front door and rang the bell.

Julian answered the door, looking like he'd just rolled out of bed in sweats and a rumpled T-shirt. His hair was in danger of being inhabited by birds. "Um...hi?"

"Hello, dear. I hope we didn't wake you."

"No, I...I was up. Kinda. I guess y'all wanna come in."

His lack of manners was no surprise, but Skye had to stop herself from giving him a hug as she passed him in the doorway. She'd never seen anyone more in need of a hug than him.

"Oh, I've always loved this house." Her momma looked around. "Are your brothers home, dear? I have an invitation for all of you."

"No idea. I'll check." Julian walked out, leaving them standing in the front room.

"How unfortunate that we woke him up. But it is after noon."

Skye hummed in agreement.

After a few minutes, Julian came back followed by Reid and Hunter.

"Mrs. Jones, Skye. You look mighty pretty this morning. Please, have a seat." Hunter, unlike his younger brother had no problems using the manners he'd been taught. "Can I get you something to drink?"

"No, thank you. We just came by to...oh, is Cameron here?"

"Not at the moment, I'm afraid. I don't know where he's off to."

"I'll call him," Reid offered.

Skye listened to her momma make small talk with Hunter while Julian clearly struggled to stay awake, leaning against the doorframe and rubbing his bloodshot eyes. Reid came back with a handful of mugs, the coffee pot in the other, and the message that Cameron would be there in a couple of minutes. Judging by the satisfied smile on her momma's face, Skye gathered she was pretty happy that she would get the full reaction of her invitation. Her mother had a big heart, a gentle soul, but she wasn't a saint.

\* \* \* \*

Cameron reckoned he owed Reid a beer. Hell, a case of beer was probably more appropriate, if not his firstborn. On his Sunday morning walk—the house was big, but sometimes he felt like the walls were closing in around him—he'd gotten coffee and was familiarizing himself with Maeville again when he'd run into Rob.

They'd been classmates growing up, but like with everyone else, Cameron had lost contact with him when he'd left town. So they had been catching up when the question came that had made Cameron break out in cold sweat.

"Say, how about you perform down at the bar sometime? I'll get you a prime Saturday night slot. I can't pay you what you're used to, of course, but your hometown hasn't seen you strut your stuff yet. What do you say?"

The truth was ruled out pretty quickly. But what lie could he come up with? That was when Reid called and saved him from answering Rob. "Sorry, man. I'm needed at home. I'll see you around."

He'd fled. Cameron could admit that. Fled right into something that was almost as bad. Maybe even worse—his ex-girlfriend's momma asking him over for Thanksgiving dinner.

"I really hope you'll all come," Mrs. Jones told Cameron and his three equally flabbergasted brothers.

"Sorry, I've got plans," Straw said, recovering first. "Ma'am." He walked out without another word. The kid was all manners and charm.

Cameron tried to catch Skye's gaze, but she just stood smiling serenely next to her excited momma. Reid made up some story about going to Ashville for the long weekend since the mill was closed. Claimed he and some friends were going waterfall rappelling and canyoning, which actually did sound like his adrenaline junkie of a brother, so maybe it was true. That left Hunter and Cameron.

"I appreciate the invitation, Mrs. Jones," Hunter said. "Really I do. I just don't think I'd be very good company. Holidays are hard."

"More reason to spend it with someone," Mrs. Jones insisted.

"I won't subject you to my bad mood, but thank you for thinking of me."

"I understand." Then she turned her gaze on Cameron. "You'll come, won't you?"

"It's best if I don't." Cameron smiled to take the sting out of his words, but kept his gaze on Mrs. Jones rather than Skye. He didn't want to see the relief he was sure he'd find on her face. She couldn't really want to spend Thanksgiving with him, but was graceful enough to go along with her mother's wishes. "You're an extraordinary woman, Mrs. Jones, I always knew that. And don't think I don't appreciate the invitation, but I think I'll keep Hunter company. Catch up on work or something."

"You stubborn boys," Mrs. Jones said. The affection was clear in her voice, however, and Cameron wanted to hug her. He hadn't declined the invitation for his own sake, nor for hers. It was with surprise he discovered that spending Thanksgiving with the Joneses was exactly what he wanted. He'd declined for Skye's sake. She shouldn't have an awkward holiday just because he was needy for family. He had his own, so he'd probably be smarter working on his own family than invading her happy one.

"She's something else," Hunter said when the Jones women had left. "I don't think I know anyone with a bigger heart except maybe Camille."

"Or Skye." Cameron wasn't sure he'd meant to say it out loud.

"Or Skye," Hunter agreed then looked at Cameron with an odd smile. "So you're keeping me company on Thanksgiving, huh? Catching up on work?"

"Oh, shut up. What the hell was I supposed to say? It was more believable than me saying I was going with Reid waterfall rappelling. Who the hell does that anyway?"

"Our brother apparently. Except he better stay home until we find out if we can just up and leave for a long weekend while still meeting the conditions of Daddy's will." Hunter grabbed his sweater and pulled it over his head. "And it's okay. I don't mind being your excuse. You can make me a turkey sandwich."

"Yeah, I'll do that." Cameron watched Hunter start to leave. "Hey, Hunt?"

"What?"

"I didn't know about your momma. I'm really sorry."

Hunter stuck his hands in his pockets and stared at the floor. "Thanks. She, uh…it was cancer. Last year. She didn't want me to know, but I got to spend the last couple of weeks with her."

"That's something at least."

"Yeah." Hunter cleared his throat. "How'd you find out?"

Cameron wasn't about to admit he'd been told off by Skye. "The bible. I suppose one of us should…update it. I figured you'd want to do it?"

"I did it last year. Daddy said it was only right. You do it this time. I'm heading out to the mill to do maintenance on the logging trucks. Someone said the scrag mill was acting up, too."

"I'll help. I've messed around with the scrag before."

"Haven't we all? I guess we should have a budget meeting and see if we can agree on replacing it."

"First we need to agree on having the meeting."

Hunter barked out a laugh. "It's going to be a long year."

A little bit of the ease from their childhood returned as Cameron and Hunter spent the rest of the Sunday working at the otherwise empty sawmill. Cameron hadn't realized how much he'd missed it. How much he'd missed Hunter.

\* \* \* \*

Thanksgiving passed quietly. Skye and her daddy had their own Black Friday at the clinic with a long queue of people who'd eaten too much turkey with all the trimmings, which kept Skye almost busy enough that she had no time to think about Cameron. Almost. She'd been so content with her life before he'd showed back up in town, never thinking she needed any more than she had. Now she spent entirely too much time wondering how he was doing, why he was keeping secrets from everyone, and why on earth she wasn't smart enough to keep herself from falling back into his web.

She didn't even enjoy the fall season the same way she usually did. The time leading up to Halloween, then Thanksgiving, and finally Christmas was her favorite time of year. This year, however, time just slipped through her fingers without her getting the same enjoyment out of it as she used to. Camille noticed, too.

"You're...off."

"Off?" They were having lunch, Camille having made the drive into town on her lunch break, and Skye's thoughts had been a million miles away.

"Decidedly off. What's wrong?"

Skye stabbed her salad without eating. "Nothing. Well, not nothing. I'm antsy. I'm never antsy."

"I guess I know why. When we were kids, I heard one of the teachers at school say that whenever something was wrong, Madigan was the reason. Those boys raised hell, didn't they? It's the same now."

"Am I that transparent?" Skye put her fork down. "And why, if they're such trouble, do we want them?"

"Beats me. All I know is that they're miserable. Hunter works around the clock, Cameron too most of the time. Reid swaggers around pretending to be in charge, but he gets this faraway look in his eyes when he thinks no one's watching, like he's looking for a horizon that isn't there. And don't get me started on Julian...that boy is so messed up he doesn't know up from down. When he's not showing up for work buzzed, he looks like he's trying to set a world record in hangovers. I don't know which is worse. He's going to hurt himself one day, working with the saws or the vehicles drunk."

"Does Hunter know?"

"I think so, but not from me. I know it's escalating, but it feels wrong to tattle on one boss to another."

"You're also friends with both of them. Well, as much as Julian lets anyone be a friend to him."

"I know. Maybe sometime when we're not at work."

Skye nodded. "I'll talk to Hunter, but you should add your two cents. I don't know if Cam told him about the day I found Julian outside town drunk. They may all be owners, bosses, whatever, but Hunter is the one we know is responsible."

Camille hummed in agreement. "Responsible isn't the first word that comes to mind with Reid and Cameron, although I have to give Cam that he's working every bit as hard as Hunter is, and he's interested in getting to know the whole operation. He doesn't act like a spoiled star just waiting to skip town again."

There would be no Best Friend of the Year Award for Skye; she'd known that for a long time. It had taken years before she'd told Camille a little bit about her secret songwriting career, but she'd never shared what she knew about Cameron's time in Nashville. Maybe it was to spare him, maybe it was to spare Camille the disappointment Skye had felt herself when she found out.

"He's different than I expected," Camille continued. "I guess I thought he'd become stuck up in all his fame and success, but he's not. Quite the opposite, in fact."

"What do we really know of his success?"

"Not much, I suppose. But people talk about his shows and his interviews and record deal. They'd have to know from somewhere. I don't really follow the music scene that closely. You'd know, though, right? Through your contacts or whatever."

"Yeah." Skye forced out a small smile, feeling like a complete fraud. That she was lying to her best friend for Cam's sake was just further proof of how far up the creek she was without a paddle. Well, up the river. The Madigan River.

Calling her daddy and saying she'd be late returning to the clinic, she got a lift with Camille out to the mill.

It was high time someone did something about Julian. He could get killed operating a saw while under the influence of alcohol or drugs.

Naturally, because she'd hoped for the opposite, Cameron was the first person she saw when she got out of the car. His logger look had always been her favorite, jeans hugging some of his best attributes, worn work boots, a red-checkered shirt, and a sweater that had seen better days. The look just worked for him like a uniform on other men. His hair was in a tight knot, and the smile he sent her very nearly made her forget that six years of being apart had passed since the last time she'd come out to the mill and seen him like this.

"Beautiful Skye. What are you doing out here? And in scrubs. Any emergencies I haven't heard about?"

"I hope not. I just came out to…" How unfair that she had to actually be able to remember why the hell she was there, or even where there was when he was looking at her like that? Like he wanted to devour her right on the spot. Cameron Madigan had devouring down to an art.

"Yes?" he prodded, smirk in place, probably totally aware of his effect on her.

"Um…Hunter. I came out to talk to Hunter."

The smirk faded from his face. Served him right.

"He's supervising over there where they're loading an order onto the trucks."

Skye turned her head to look. Maybe he wasn't going to be pleased about her interrupting his work, but she didn't have all day to wait around, and out of the corner she could see Julian working with she was relatively sure was some sort of debarking machine.

She wished she had the authority to do a blood test on him. Not to get him in trouble but to keep him safe. Safe from himself.

When she looked back at Cameron, he was already several yards away. She ran to catch up with him. It involved him, too. "Actually, if you're not busy, I'd like you to be there, too."

He masked the surprise quickly but not before she saw it. He shrugged. "Sure."

# Chapter Nine

"What?" Hunter snapped in annoyance when Skye called his name. When he saw it was her, the irritation on his face disappeared. "Sorry, I didn't realize it was you. Reid's been bugging me all day, asking me questions about everything like he's never set foot here before. What are you doing here?"

"I need to talk to you. And Cam."

"All right."

Skye looked around, knowing Julian wasn't far away. The guilt started to gnaw at her, but she was going behind his back for his own safety. "Not here."

"Daddy's office. Well, our office." Hunter led the way, and Skye followed with Cameron trailing behind.

"Something wrong? I don't suppose you want to place an order." Hunter headed toward the coffee machine and poured three cups without asking if anyone wanted any.

Skye waited until Cameron had closed the door behind them. She'd never been inside the office before, only outside in the reception area where Camille reigned. It was an honest reflection of the man who'd designed and used it—dark wood, drenched in masculinity, and a desk as large and ostentatious as the big, gleaming truck that sat unused in the driveway outside the house on Madigan Avenue. Though an honest, hardworking man, Thomas Madigan had liked to flaunt his success.

"You'll probably both say it's none of my business, but I'm worried about Julian." Skye paced, hands wrapped around the warm cup of coffee.

Perched against the desk, Hunter looked at Cameron, who was sitting in one of the visitor's chairs with his right ankle resting on his left knee. "What do you mean?" he asked Skye.

"You know what I mean." She looked at Cameron. "Did you tell him about the day I brought Julian home?"

"I'm not his momma. Kid's old enough to do what he wants and face whatever consequences that brings him."

Skye rolled her eyes. "One's ignorant and the other simply doesn't care. Listen, I know it's not something y'all want on the front page of The Maeville Gazette, but people already know. You think there isn't talk in town about how the youngest Madigan gets drunk or high and is mixed up with a bad crowd? It's not something you can hide by sticking your head in the sand. And yes, Cam, he's old enough to make his own choices and face the consequences of those. But the fact of the matter is that he's working here every day using heavy machinery and dangerous tools. He's endangering his health, his life, and possibly the lives of those he works with. More than that...can't you see he's hurting? My heart breaks just looking at him."

"Shit." Cam sprang up and went to refill his cup. "You're right, okay? But what the hell are we supposed to do about it? He sneers at everything anyone says to him, and he has to work here."

"It's gotten worse since Daddy died. They fought like cats and dogs, but..." Hunter sighed. "I tried to help him when it started to escalate, but he resented me for it. Said I was doing it just to show Daddy I was better than him. I don't know what we can do when he doesn't want to be helped. And Cam's right, we can't just boot him back to his fishing boat. He has to work here or the conditions of the will aren't met and the others lose their inheritance."

"There has to be a way to get through to him," Skye insisted.

"Yeah, beat him senseless."

"You're not helping, Cam."

Cameron shrugged and sat back down.

"Ganging up on him won't help, and neither will anything I say," Hunter said thoughtfully. "My best bet is one of you. He might not sneer so much at you, Skye. He might sneer plenty at Cam, but it's possible he'll listen to you anyway when he remembers it's possible to come from sleepy old Maeville and still make something of yourself."

"Let Skye do it," Cameron said quickly.

"It will sound better coming from you," Skye argued although she knew why Cameron wanted to avoid it. "Julian could, with good reason, tell me it's none of my business. He can't do that with you because y'all have a stock in what happens here at the sawmill."

"I think she's right," Hunter said to Cameron.

"Great. Just great. Y'all are worried about Straw, but I'm the one who has to talk to him."

"Aren't you worried about him, too?" Skye asked.

"Of course I am. Shit. But when I was his age, I was on my own without anyone worrying about how I was doing or if I was getting in trouble. Kid's gotta learn how to be an adult."

"That's not Julian's fault."

"No." Cameron sneered. "Nothing is poor little Strawberry's fault."

"With that attitude, it's probably better if you don't talk to him." Skye turned to Hunter. "If you want me to do it, or if I can help in some other way, let me know."

Neither of the men acknowledged her leaving, but the moment she closed the door, the shouting started. Perhaps she'd just wasted her own time as well as theirs. All they did was yell, and *that* she knew would not help Julian.

Instead of going out the side door, she walked down the short hallway and out into Camille's domain. Her friend was bent over her desk, sorting through a stack of papers. When she heard Skye, she looked up. "Any luck?"

"I don't think so." Skye perched on the edge of Camille's desk. "It's not that they don't understand the problem, but since there are no obvious ways to solve it, they'd rather just yell at each other and blame Julian for his own problems."

"Men."

Skye smiled wryly. "Yep."

"There's a truck leaving in a couple of minutes if you want a lift back into town. I told Reid to wait for you."

"Thanks. I'll catch you later."

During the short drive into town, Skye debated whether or not to try her luck talking to Reid about Julian, but she decided against it. She didn't know him as well as she knew Cameron and Hunter, or even Julian, because he'd been gone longer, and he didn't seem like the most responsible of the brothers although he was perhaps the most friendly and easygoing. Instead she just listened to his jokes and wondered what to do about the fact that she'd seen Cameron less than ten minutes ago and she was already missing him, sour face and all.

* * * *

"All right, all right, I'll talk to him, but we both know he won't hear a word I say." Cameron heaved himself up from the chair. "What was that you said about his fishing boat?"

"Up river. He hasn't been working here as much as he's been fishing since…well, since finishing high school actually. He and Daddy never got along." Hunter went to refill his cup for the third time. "There's a crew up there who goes out pound net fishing every morning. Not the idiots he wastes time with in town, but decent fellas who work hard and stay out of trouble."

That was good news in Cameron's ears. It meant that Straw wasn't a completely lost cause, who was only hell bent on self-destruction. "I'll talk to him," he said and left the office.

The rest of the day he wondered how to approach his brother. The more he thought about it, the more he realized how right Skye was. It was dangerous, not just for Straw but for everyone, to have him working at the mill if he was drunk or high. The fact that Skye cared so much didn't surprise him. It wasn't because of him, that much he was sure of, and it couldn't be because she was such good friends with Straw, either. The kid made that impossible with his miserable attitude.

So it had to be because of her friendship with Hunter and because she just had that big a heart and caring nature. As much as he thought she was wasting her time nursing instead of writing songs, her profession fit her. It was weird, though. Back when Cameron had dated her, she hadn't been best pals with his brothers. They'd been friendly enough, but the only thing she and Hunter had had in common was him. Now they seemed to have all kinds of stuff in common, and although he wasn't going to admit it to anyone, he could be honest with himself. He was jealous.

An opportunity to talk to Straw didn't arise until late that night. The kid disappeared from the sawmill, skipped the dinner Cameron painstakingly cooked because he hadn't been able to convince anyone that it wasn't his turn, and didn't come home until late. But Cameron was waiting for him in the front room, relaxing to the sound of Reid bitching about having to do the dishes. It almost sounded like he enjoyed it.

"Dude. Why are you sitting here in the dark? It's creepy," Straw complained when he spotted Cameron.

"Enjoying life. Just listen."

Straw was silent for a moment. "All I can hear is Reid complaining about the dishes."

"Exactly. Means he's doing them and I'm not."

Straw snorted. "Nice."

"I was going to ask you to come out for a beer, but it's a bit late now. How about a night cap courtesy of Daddy's liquor cabinet?"

"Why?" Suspicion laced Straw's tone.

Cameron rose. "Just thought I'd put a little effort into actually having a real conversation with you. We haven't had one yet, but I'm feeling hopeful as I think I had what passes as a conversation with Hunter the other day. Now I just need to have one with you and Reid, and I pass the brother exam."

Straw hesitated while Cameron held his breath. He'd decided to add as little pressure as possible, thinking pressure was a sure way to make Straw bail. And it wasn't a complete lie. Cameron would love to have an actual conversation with his youngest brother, who'd always been just that tad too young to bother with. He'd asked himself if doing it over a drink was the best course of action when the point was to get Straw cut back on his drinking. And no, it wasn't smart, but Cameron needed all the help he could get.

"The liquor cabinet is empty," Straw said at last.

"I know." And Straw had probably been the one to empty it. "We'll just have to hope the secret one isn't."

"There's a secret liquor cabinet?"

It was sad that it took a secret stash of booze to get rid of the sneers, the suspicion, and the hate in Straw's voice. "Yep."

"Why didn't I know about that?"

"How the hell should I know? I saw it years ago when I was still in high school and hovering outside Daddy's office door trying to find the courage to go in and show him a not very impressive report card."

"Well, let's go."

Cameron led the way to the office, hoping Hunter wasn't holed up in there. It was strange; every time he went in there he almost expected to find his daddy still behind the desk looking up with annoyance at being interrupted.

Thankfully the office was empty, and Cameron headed for the panel he'd seen opened once. He hadn't thought about it in years, never tried to open it, but counted himself lucky he'd thought of it when he needed an in with Straw. If it had to be alcohol, then so be it. Lure the kid with alcohol to make him stop drinking. It was sad it was the best Cameron could come up with.

"Is there a lock?" Straw asked, looking over Cameron's shoulder.

"No idea." It took him a few minutes, but eventually he found a pressure mechanism and the panel opened up, revealing the finest of liquors. Mentally, he reminded himself to clear out the cabinet and hide the bottles somewhere else. He hoped Straw would listen, but he wasn't expecting miracles.

"Sweet."

Drinking whiskey older than both of them, they sat in each their deep armchair. Silence reigned, and Cameron didn't know how to start, afraid he'd blow it.

"So, what do brothers talk about?" Straw asked eventually.

"Sad you have to ask when you've got three of them." Cameron enjoyed the smooth burn down his throat as he sipped the whiskey. "And just as sad that I don't have a clue, either."

"Silence isn't so bad."

Cameron had come to the same conclusion in the past few years. "No, it isn't. I do have something specific I want to talk to you about, though. Working at the mill under the influence isn't okay, and I'd like for you to stop doing it. Not for my sake, not for Hunter or Reid's, but for your sake. You'll end up getting hurt, and I don't want that."

"Why?" Straw looked him in the eye and drank from his tumbler. "What difference does it make to you whether or not I get hurt?"

It wasn't the reaction Cameron had expected. Who was the stranger in front of him? "I just realized that we don't know each other at all. That means you don't have to believe when I say it's because I care, but it's true. I haven't acted like family matters lately, but I guess it does. I don't want my brother to get hurt."

"That's right. You haven't acted like you care." Straw rose and filled his glass. Instead of sitting back down, he saluted Cameron. "Cheers and thanks for the talk. I didn't realize what I'd been missing."

He left, and Cameron refilled his glass, too. That had backfired like he'd expected all along, but it hadn't backfired the way he'd thought it would. Straw wasn't just a snotty brat with a chip on his shoulder and a bucket load of self-pity. He was a genuinely broken man who looked at life through very cynical glasses. Cameron was at a loss for what to do for him — what to do about him.

\* \* \* \*

"I struck out."

Skye looked up from the computer screen at the clinic and saw Cameron standing hipshot in front of the reception desk. With the Stetson and the vest over his shirt, he looked like he'd just come in from the range. She wondered if he'd notice if she checked her chin for drool. "Huh?"

"I struck out," he repeated. "With Straw. I think the hurt runs deeper than I'd expected. I tried not to put pressure on him or blame him, but he still saw right through me and bailed."

"Um…" Skye looked around, grateful it was so late in the day that the waiting room was empty. But her daddy was still there, busy with the last patient. "Why don't we get out of here? The mayor's wife's in with Daddy, and while she insists she never gossips, she likes few things better than to pass on news. I don't want her to overhear anything about Julian."

"All right."

"I'll just write a note." Quickly scribbling a note to her daddy that she had left for the day and pinning it where he'd see it, she grabbed her things and was grateful she'd already changed out of her scrubs.

"Wanna go for a cup of coffee?" Cameron asked, holding the door open for her. It was almost like the old days when he'd pick her up at the clinic or at school, taking her out for a little while before they parted ways for dinner.

"I'd like that."

Seated across from him in the little coffee house, Skye felt as awkward as she had on their very first date when she'd been fifteen years old.

"It's weird, isn't it?" he asked, apparently thinking the same thing she was.

"A little. It's been so long."

It helped when Cameron told her about the sad excuse for a talk he'd tried to have with Julian. She wasn't overly surprised, although she'd hoped he'd be able to get through to the angry young man, who seemed to be begging for someone to give him a hug.

"I think you did what you could," Skye told Cameron. "It's naïve to expect years of anger and problems to disappear just because you try to talk to him. I don't think he'll be able to break free of his pattern of drinking and being angry on his own, so maybe the trick is to keep trying to talk to him. Which of course could be wrong, too, as that would mean pushing him. Eventually we all break."

"Sounds like there's no solution." And that looked like it might break Cameron. Skye hadn't been aware there was such a strong bond between the Madigan brothers, but what did she know? She had a brother who was there if she really needed him no matter how many days or weeks passed between their phone calls and e-mails.

"No, there is." She reached across the table and laid her hand over his. "And we'll find it. Until we do, we just make sure he knows we care."

Cameron turned his hand and laced their fingers together. "Do you think his momma screwed him up? Charlene was— well, she still is I suppose—a nightmare. She treated Straw like he was a disposable razor."

"It probably plays a part. He and your daddy had their issues, as well, as far as I understand."

Cameron nodded. "Do you think...well, did my leaving mess him up, too, you think?"

"Maybe, but if he felt abandoned, which I think we all did to be honest, then it's not your fault. He was an adult and so were you. I didn't fall to pieces when Sebastian went off to college."

It was a relief that Cameron didn't mention her comment about them all feeling a little abandoned when he'd left. She hadn't meant to say it. It was also a relief that even as their conversation drifted away from the safe topic of Julian, it flowed naturally. She'd never expected to be able to talk about everyday things with Cameron—the sawmill, the clinic, people they both knew.

The cup of coffee became two, and before she knew it, she'd agreed to have dinner with him. It was as natural as breathing, although a little voice inside of her screamed at her to be careful, danger was ahead. She decided to ignore it.

# Chapter Ten

He had ignored the stares they'd gotten at the coffee house and at the restaurant. And there had been stares. Whispers. Doc's Skye was with the Madigan boy again. Wasn't he the one who went off to become a star? Luckily, it was easy to get lost in the green eyes and tempting lips of the beautiful face across the table. Cameron was torn between losing himself in the moment and not being able to understand she was giving him the time of day. The evening flew by even as he tried to savor every moment like a thirsty man who was given a thimble of water after too long in the desert.

"Thanks for dinner. It's not how I'd envisioned my night to go, but I'm glad for the change in plans." Skye smiled at him as she slung her scarf around her neck outside the restaurant.

There was an ache in Cameron's chest, one caused by the knowledge that they'd be parting soon, and maybe once the harsh light of day returned, everything would be back to normal where they argued every other time they saw each other.

"How about a nightcap?" he blurted before he'd thought it through.

She glanced across the street to the only decent bar in town. "Do you think that's wise?"

"Sure. Why not?"

"Well, because I got a text from Camille earlier. She, along with the usual crowd we hang out with over there once or twice a week, is there now. Hunter's probably there. People have stared and whispered tonight, but that's nothing compared to what will happen if we walk in there."

"All right. I'll walk you home then. Unless you're afraid someone might look out the window and see us together."

"Cam, that's not what I meant. But you know Maeville, in fact you know it so well that you left it behind. I don't think we need the pressure."

"And now I'm back," he said, at the moment resigned to the fact, as they started walking. He hadn't wanted to walk into that bar and see Hunter anymore than she had, but not for the same reason. He didn't want to share her. It stung that she just didn't like being seen with him.

"Yes, you are." Her tone was flat, and the ease between them from earlier faded away in the cool night air.

Maeville wasn't a bustling metropolis in the evenings. They saw three cars and met a man walking his dog. Much too soon, or not soon enough—Cameron couldn't quite decide after the turn the mood had taken—they reached Skye's cabin. It had belonged to a logger's widow once, but Skye had breathed life back into it judging by the look of it from the outside. A welcoming light shone beside the front door, which was decorated with a fall wreath. Pots of heather cluttered the porch charmingly.

"Thanks for tonight, Cam."

"Yeah. Thanks. It's been a while since I enjoyed dinner as much as I did tonight."

"I didn't mean to offend you. I'm not ashamed to be seen with you, but I'm not going to be the reason you run again. The pressure got to you as much your dreams, didn't it?"

He shifted his weight from one foot to the other. She had him figured out a lot more than he felt comfortable with. "Maybe."

She smiled. "How about that nightcap?"

Surprised, he nodded and followed her inside. He'd probably agree to strolling through hell if she asked, though being invited inside was more like visiting heaven. If heaven was anything like the slightly bohemian palace Skye had made for herself. It was kind of like Arabian Nights meeting The Little House on the Prairie. And for some reason it worked. Cameron felt instantly at home, though maybe that had more to do with the owner of cabin than its décor.

The ease returned. Maybe they were just better when they focused on each other rather than on the rest of the world. And with the rest of the world locked safely out, town gossip and the wind that started howling around the cabin corners unable to touch them, neither of them stopped to question the transition from drinks on the couch to being lip-locked and heading toward the stairs. They'd been sitting close on the couch, the drinks and the candlelight apparently getting to them. Cameron had no real explanation except maybe that need and want had overwhelmed him. Overwhelmed her. Overwhelmed them. Maybe because it had never really gone away even though six long years had passed.

Cameron had been dreaming of Skye ever since he'd been foolish enough to leave her. He thought he'd been good at keeping the memory of her alive in his mind, but that theory had been blown to pieces the first time he'd seen her again.

She'd been more beautiful than he remembered. It was the same with her taste—it exploded on his tongue and taunted him for thinking Skye Jones was a woman he could survive without. She had to be tasted, felt, breathed, experienced, or a man was effectively reduced to dust without her. Cameron had been nothing but dust blowing in the wind in Nashville. He hadn't been really alive, not even coming close to feeling like the man he felt under her touch.

"Skye…" Her name was a prayer on his lips.

They stumbled on the stairs, Cameron's hip and elbow receiving the brunt force of their fall. He knew he was supposed to feel a little pain, but all he felt was Skye. The small interruption in their stride gave him a moment to wonder if they were about to make a mistake.

"Stop thinking," Skye told him as if she could read his mind. He wouldn't be surprised if she could. She eclipsed his entire world, became the sun, the moon, and the stars on a sky that had been dark for too long. He grabbed the back of her head and fused their lips together almost violently. She was right. No more thinking.

* * * *

Skye was drowning in a sea of the passion she'd been searching for since the last time she'd been in Cameron's arms, the kind of passion she wanted to knead into her songs and walk to work every morning whistling because of. Damn Cameron Madigan for being the only one able to give it to her. And bless him for reentering her life and reigniting a flame that had been extinct too long.

In the light from the bedside lamp she'd nearly knocked over when trying to turn it on, his face was half-hidden in shadows as he rested his weight on top of her. Clothes gone, ripped off or incinerated due to the intense heat they created together, Skye had no idea. But the feel of him—the full feel of him—again was so overwhelming she felt reborn, her body full of star shine and moon glow. She arched her back and closed her eyes as his large, work-roughened hands slid down her body. He'd always been able to play her as expertly as he played the guitar. She gasped. And he had an excellent memory, remembering exactly how to make her quiver and her blood sing. It was possible they had never been more in tune.

"Beautiful Skye."

The breathless whisper against her throat made Skye shiver. Then he made them spiral together toward the stars, sending her momentarily into a void where nothing existed except the drum of her pulse and her nerve endings paying homage to the man who lay heavily on top of her. She wished he'd never move.

No words were spoken. Skye felt that even a whisper would break the spell they were both under, and she wasn't ready for that. She knew what she would feel as soon as she let herself, and the only way to enjoy the moment was to ignore the future, even if it was just minutes or hours away. Sleep found them as they lay wrapped around each other, a preferred way of sleeping they hadn't forgotten.

Twice during the night they woke to set fire to the sheets and to Skye's heart, whose beat became more and more painful. Oblivion took them twice.

How they'd ever been able to stay away from each other, or make civil conversation as if the magic they created together as soon as the lights were out and the clothes were off would never happen again, was beyond her.

There was no home for her except the one she found in Cameron's arms, no fire to ignite her but the one he lit, no reason to wake up in the morning but to see his smile. She wanted forever, but even just tomorrow was probably asking for too much.

The last time they drifted off was just before dawn. Skye knew their time was limited, so she snuggled even closer to the hard, warm body beside her. The way he tightened his arms around her made her suspect that he knew it, too.

When she woke up again, it was to a whisper in her ear and an empty bed beside her. "Skye? I have to go. I promised Hunter I'd come to the mill early and help him with some orders. I'll find you later, okay?"

Not fully awake yet, she sighed as his lips skimmed her temple. Sighed again as his touch vanished. Blinked her eyes open a moment later when she heard the front door. The events of last night rolled through her mind in waves, making her body tingle as if Cameron was still there. But he wasn't. He'd left, and as she sat up and reached for her robe in the dim morning light, she decided that it was probably for the best. Not in any rush as it was still early, she went into the kitchen and saw coffee already made. She poured a cup and moved over to look out the window. A grey day was ahead it seemed. Dull. Everything her night with Cameron hadn't been.

It was a conundrum how something so wrong could feel so fantastic. They'd done nothing wrong, had hurt no one but possibly themselves later on, yet it was wrong on every level. The most amazing night she'd had in more than half a decade had been the biggest mistake she could remember making. Because now she'd reminded herself of how good they were together, of how much more of herself he made her feel, and exactly how much she still loved him. How much she'd always loved him and always would. It had been so blissful to be ignorant.

Because it couldn't happen again. She hadn't spent all this time making herself into the kind of person she wanted to be only to let Cameron shuffle back into town and ruin everything. Even if he was what she wanted, he definitely wasn't what she needed. Once he'd had the power to break her into a million pieces. She'd given him that power willingly, truly believing he'd never use it. But he had. And although she made mistakes, she was determined never to make the same one twice. Except...last night was evidence of the opposite.

Careful not to let her thoughts wander down paths she was determined to ignore until she felt in complete control of herself, Skye showered, dressed, and got ready for work. In some ways she didn't feel like the same woman who had left the clinic the previous afternoon, but she had to be the same daughter and the same nurse who returned to work. Her daddy knew her well, and Maeville was full of people who'd not only known her since she'd been born, but also loved to gossip. She had experienced their relentlessness before, and she was in no mood for it today.

* * * *

Cameron whistled as he moved pallets with the forklift. He'd forgotten how much more enjoyable work was when you had something nice to think about as you did the manual labor. He continued whistling until Hunter stopped covering the stacks of pallets with tarps and looked at him.

"I'll pretend I didn't notice that you didn't come home last night if you stop doing that. You could at least sing and give us a free concert. Your whistling's shit."

"Why do you have to pretend? We're all adults." The singing comment, as well as the realization of what he'd been doing soured his mood slightly.

"I don't know how breaking up with Skye affected you because you weren't around, but I know how it affected her. She's a good friend who I care a lot about. I'd hate to see her messed up again."

"You don't know anything."

Hunter shrugged. "No more than half the town who's busy talking about you two."

Cameron was in no mood to listen to Hunter go into protective big brother mode on Skye's behalf. So he jumped down from the forklift and left. There was bound to be some work somewhere that didn't include Hunter's presence. Goddamn know-it-all. It was hell to hear that Skye had been messed up after he'd left. Cameron knew he'd hurt her, but he didn't need Hunter telling him about it. Skye seemed to have somewhat forgiven him, so why the hell couldn't his brother?

Since the excellent mood he'd started the day out with was gone, he went ahead and examined why he'd been whistling as he grabbed the lopping shears and headed toward the job no one wanted: cutting down holly in what they called the Christmas orchard.

He'd made a promise to himself about music. He'd never sing another tune, never strum his guitar, never participate in anything even remotely related to music. He hadn't whistled or voluntarily listened to the radio in two years. He'd listened to music, but only in places where he couldn't avoid it or had no control over it. Now it was like one night with Skye was making the music bubble back up inside of him. As much as he wanted her, and good lord he wanted her, she wasn't supposed to have that much power. When it came to music, he didn't want anything to rock the boat. It was a closed chapter of his life.

He considered heading into town for lunch but decided he'd rather finish up early and go find her then. Maybe they'd have dinner out again, maybe they'd eat in. Yes, eat in, he thought to himself, that was by far the best idea.

It was like she'd breathed life back into him, he reflected as he cut down holly branches and ignored the light drizzle. She was good for him, and so was, he admitted with only a little reluctance, Maeville—the fresh air, the slow pace, the forest, and the river. He felt revitalized. Alive. And that was so soon after coming back as an empty shell compared to the man he used to be.

A little voice in the back of his head told him that there were a few things he was forgetting, such as the deceptive cloak he was still wearing, and the fact that his daddy had just died.

Cameron didn't know what to do about the lies and the deception. He didn't know how to handle admitting the truth any less than he knew how to grieve for a man he'd lost six years ago.

The light drizzle had picked up, and Cameron was drenched to the bone by the time he heard a truck rumble down the rarely-used track. He stopped what he was doing, wiped a dirty work glove over his forehead, and watched Reid jumped down from the truck.

"Hunter sent me down here. Well, after he and Straw argued for almost twenty minutes who'd go pick you up. What did you do to offend them?"

"Mind your own business and help me with these." Cameron started picking up the branches he'd cut. There'd be enough for the Christmas markets and for the Christmas tree team to take into town to sell along with the trees. The local ladies they'd hired to make wreaths had already come down to cut their own holly.

"Yes, boss."

"Shut up."

They loaded the truck, quietly grumbling when the pointy leaves scratched their skin. Cutting down holly was a small task, but everyone hated it.

"You missed your turn with the dishes last night," Reid said, reaching into the cab for two water bottles and throwing one to Cameron, who almost caught it.

"Says who? It can't possibly be my turn to do the dishes when I'm not there for dinner."

Reid shrugged. "It's your turn when someone says it's your turn. Swim or sink in the Madigan household, sonny. But don't worry, they're waiting for you at home. We wouldn't dream of taking your dirty dishes away from you."

"Fuck that. I'm not doing them."

"Spending the night at Skye's again tonight?"

Cameron emptied the bottle greedily. "How the hell does everyone know where I am every single second of the day? And, more importantly, why do you seem to think it's any of your damn business?"

"Welcome back to Maeville, Cam. Remember why we left?" Cackling, Reid climbed into the truck. "Coming?"

"No, I'll walk."

"Suit yourself." Reid drove off, the truck bouncing around on the uneven path.

Cameron kicked the nearest tree. Damn fucking town and the people in it for ruining his perfect mood. It just figured that as soon as he found a little respite from the relentlessness of life, someone had to be an ass about it. It was likely the gossip would spook Skye as well. He checked his watch. It was only a little after three, but he didn't care. He'd go home, grab a shower and some dry clothes, and then he was heading over to the clinic to see Skye. Let Reid deal with the holly and Hunter deal with...everything else. That's how Hunter preferred it anyway. If he didn't do something himself, he was looking over the shoulder of the person who did. As if he was the only one who knew what he was doing just because he'd never done anything with his life expect work at the mill. Screw him. And screw everyone else along with him.

Cameron sighed, turning his face upward and letting the rain wash away the petulant four-year-old he'd apparently turned into.

# Chapter Eleven

"Okay, out with it. What's eating you today?"

Skye looked up from the computer screen she'd been staring at without seeing the journal she'd pulled up. Her daddy was looking at her, eyebrows raised. "Nothing. I'm fine."

"Skye."

She sighed. "Okay, maybe I'm a little tired."

"This father knows his daughter a little better than that," her daddy told her. "But have it your way. I called your momma. She's coming in this afternoon, so you can head home and catch up on your sleep."

She straightened her back, annoyed that she actually felt guilty. "That's not necessary. I can do my job."

"Without doubt."

"Daddy, come on. I'll go grab a cup of coffee, and then I'll be fine. Promise."

"Go home. Your head's not in the game today, honey."

He was right, of course, but she hated admitting it. Even to herself. With a shake of her head, she rose from the chair and went to grab her things. Continuing to argue wouldn't do her any good—the doctor was known for his stubbornness, and although she'd inherited the trait, her own stubbornness was no match for her daddy's.

She went home to a house where everything suddenly reminded her of Cameron, although he'd only been there once. He was a ghost haunting her. When she'd changed into some comfortable sweats, she settled down to put some of the emotions swimming around inside of her down on paper. If nothing else, her mistake might get twisted into a song. But of course she couldn't settle. Restless, she sprang back up and started pacing her living room—her comfortable, inspiring living room she'd designed with relaxation in mind. She groaned. Was mindless pleasure worth it when you felt like you didn't belong in your own body the next day?

Abandoning her songwriting, she turned on some music—one of the many artists she'd written for—and went into the kitchen to inspect the cabinets. Then breathed a sigh of relief. She wasn't a completely hopeless case yet—she had all the ingredients for brownies and a tub of homemade vanilla ice cream in the freezer. Dinner of champions and emotional females. She immediately got to work.

Skye had gotten to the important task of licking the spoon when the doorbell rang. She put the spoon down but hesitated going to the door. There was every chance it was Cameron, and she wasn't at all sure opening the door for him was a good idea. She'd already proved she had absolutely no self-respect when it came to him. She was so weak she might throw herself at him.

The bell rang out again. Of course, it could also be Camille. Or maybe her momma who'd caught a case of the worries from her daddy. Or it could be Hunter. He'd been known to stop by with a load of firewood and a pizza from time to time, though not since Cameron had come back to town.

It could also be freaking Santa Claus lost on his way to the North Pole, and she wasn't going to satisfy her curiosity standing around with a half-licked spoon.

Before she reached the front door, the bell rang out a third time. Whoever was outside wasn't taking no for an answer. She had no peephole, but she could see Cameron clearly through the window when she went through the living room. It just had to be him. She'd expected it, and an annoying part of her had hoped it.

Skye opened the door. "Hi."

He gave her an odd stare. "Do I want to know what that brown stuff on your face is?"

A snort escaped her, and she looked in the mirror above the small dresser next to the door. She had brownie batter on her nose and on her cheek. She wiped it off with her finger and licked it clean. "Brownie batter. No one was around to fight me for the spoon."

"Crap. Guess I got here a few minutes too late."

"Guess you did." She wandered back to the kitchen, knowing he'd follow. There was no going back to forced politeness when two people knew each other as well as they did.

"I went by the clinic. Your daddy said he'd sent you home because you were spacey."

She turned around, saw him leaning against the doorframe between the kitchen and the hallway. "Spacey? He said I was spacey?"

Cameron nodded. She was sure there was a hint of a smirk in the corner of his mouth. He'd obviously already gathered that she was *spacey* because of him. It was damn annoying, especially since it was true.

"I was tired."

"Well, you didn't get a lot of sleep, so I suppose that's understandable." He eliminated the space between them, leaning in so close she could smell he'd recently brushed his teeth. Why wasn't she moving away? When their lips met, she seemed to relax fully for the first time since she'd woken up that morning. Oh, but he was an expert kisser—had always known exactly how to make her melt into a puddle at his feet. Now was no exception, so it took a while before she'd gathered her wits enough to take a step back.

"I can't think when you do that." She turned her back to him and started rinsing out the bowl and the spoon she'd used for the batter.

"Thinking's overrated," was his obvious answer.

"No, it's not." The kitchen timer went off, but she didn't particularly feel saved by the bell. She did, however, get a moment to think while getting the brownies out of the oven. When she turned back to him, he had his arms crossed over his chest while he looked at her with a frown.

* * * *

She looked the same, tasted the same, felt the same, but something was off. "Want to clue me in on what's happened between this morning and now?" Cameron asked, annoyance at how much her behavior was affecting him probably the only thing that saved his voice from wobbling. He'd been on his own for years, but he'd never felt as lonely as he did right then.

Skye didn't meet his gaze. "Nothing."

His hand shot out to grab her chin, forcing her to look at him. "Come on, Skye. Didn't last night mean anything to you?"

She yanked her face out of his hold. "Of course it did."

"Then what's up with you now?" He hadn't often sought out female companionship in Nashville, afraid he'd be recognized and afraid that he wouldn't. And when he had, it had never been more than one-night-stands. So he'd forgotten exactly how frustrating dealing with women could be—how they sometimes seemed to be talking a different language where the words were the same but their meaning different. Men who claimed to have figured out the female mind were great big liars.

"Nothing is up," Skye claimed. She fussed around a bit, and he decided to wait her out. It took a while. First she cleaned up. Then she made coffee. All the while the brownies were right there smelling like heaven. Cameron was afraid she'd chop off his fingers if he helped himself, though, so he just watched her. When she'd finally poured two cups of coffee, she walked out of the kitchen with them.

He sighed. Damn the woman. "What about the brownies?"

"They're not for you," she called back from the living room.

So she was sadistic, too. He didn't remember that trait, meaning it had to be one she'd developed recently. Casting one last look at the cooling cake tray, he left the kitchen.

Skye was curled up on the couch cradling a coffee mug in her hands. He sat down next to her, ignoring the stupid coffee. He hadn't come for fucking coffee. "So?" he prompted her.

"Last night was heavenly, but it was also a mistake that — if we'd been smart — shouldn't have happened. Maybe it was inevitable, though." She sipped her coffee. "Maybe it was our way of getting closure."

"Are you listening to yourself?" Closure? What the hell was she talking about? Last night hadn't been even remotely about closure, quite the opposite, in fact. Something had been rekindled.

"Yes. Are you?"

She was serious. Unable to believe his ears, he jumped up and started pacing. "I can't believe that's what you got out of it. I know I blew it when I left, but we had something special. And last night we proved that we still have it. How can you turn your back on that? We could...we could be better than we were."

Skye hesitated. He could practically see the wheels in her mind turning. Lord, but she was something else. So at ease with herself, so unaware of the light that shone from her like a beacon. She wasn't just beautiful; she was otherworldly to look at sometimes, and as frustrating as nothing else he'd ever encountered. He was probably insane, but he wouldn't want her any other way. There was nothing about her that he didn't love. Hadn't loved from the moment the boy he'd used to be had looked at her one day and realized that girls weren't as icky as he'd thought. No one else had existed in his mind since, not really. Everyone else was a shadow or bad imitation of her — of the real thing.

"Do you really mean that when you're still lying to me?"

A chill ran from the tip of his toes to the top of his head. "What do you mean?"

"You know what." Her tone was neutral, but he had the feeling she possessed the power to ruin his life.

Because there was only one thing he was lying about.

He didn't have it in him to look her in the eyes. Of all the people he wished would never find out, she was at the very top of the list. To everyone else, he'd just have failed. To her, he'd have thrown away the chance of a future for the two of them together for nothing. The silence stretched uncomfortably. He wanted to say something, but not a single word was to be found in his brain.

"Maybe you should just leave," Skye suggested gently after a while. She was spinning around one of the rings on her fingers, not looking at him.

Maybe he should, only it felt like leaving her all over again, and this time it wasn't to chase anything except maybe solitude. On the other hand, there was no way he could stay when he didn't have an explanation to offer her. It wasn't even stuck in his throat; it was stuck beyond his reach.

He left. Not by choice this time but by necessity. He rubbed his chest where a dull ache throbbed as he walked out to his car. If he'd thought he knew what devastation felt like, he'd been wrong. A million crushed music dreams couldn't compare to one crushed Skye dream. And the worst of it all was that he'd done the same thing to her before.

Cameron hit the steering wheel when he got into the car. Before yesterday, he hadn't even been aware he'd wanted them to rekindle their love so badly—how desperately he needed it. But at least he knew now. He snorted and started the car. Part of him wanted to disappear, but an even bigger part of him just wanted to go home. So he did, even if it was an unfamiliar feeling.

It wasn't nearly as smart as it was predictable that he stopped for a six-pack and a bottle of cheap whiskey. Once home, he didn't get a chance to get started drinking any of it before Reid was in his face complaining about last night's dishes. Loud rock rumbled out from upstairs, where it seemed Straw was having his own party. And just as Cameron had ditched Reid and the dishes, Hunter blocked his path.

"Listen, about you and Skye—"

"Butt out," Cameron said, outmaneuvering Hunter and shutting the door to the office before he could be followed. He locked it, too.

Hunter knocked, and Straw's music floated clearly through the ceiling. Cameron groaned. If he couldn't get any peace the natural way, he supposed he might as well drink himself into a coma and find some relief that way.

* * * *

It had been the right thing to do, Skye assured herself as she scooped out a second helping of the rather excellent vanilla ice cream. The hurt was to be expected, but she'd survived it before and she would survive it again. This time she could even comfort herself with the knowledge that it was partly her own fault for being weak. Except that wasn't really a comfort at all. It had been a necessary choice to make after her momentary—a moment that lasted all night—lapse in judgment.

The phone rang as she carried her cake and ice cream to the couch. "I don't want to talk to you, Cam," she told the phone.

It rang again when she'd devoured her fourth brownie of the evening. Not long after turning eighteen, she'd decided that since she was now an adult, dessert for dinner was acceptable in crisis situations. This counted as one.

When the phone rang a third time, she leaned over to check the caller ID. Instead of Cameron's name—or "Unknown" as it might have been since she had no idea if he still had the same cell phone number—it said "Hunter." She grabbed the phone.

"Hello."

"Hi. I was beginning to think you were ignoring me."

"No, just your brother."

"Ah."

Skye pushed away her ice cream bowl. She'd had enough in more ways than one, and there really was no reason to let Cameron affect her ability to fit into the jeans she'd just bought half a size too small. "What does that mean?"

"It means that I was calling to ask if you knew why Cam's locked himself in Daddy's office with a six-pack and a bottle of whiskey, but I think you already gave me the answer."

"This is all very high school."

Hunter chuckled. "Yep. Are you okay?"

"Yeah, I'm okay." Skye eyed the ice cream. Okay, maybe not, but even though Hunter was a friend and hadn't been in regular contact with Cameron in years, they were still brothers.

"Would you tell me if you weren't?" Well, he seemed to have her number dialed.

"I don't know. There's no reason for you to get stuck in the middle between two adults who can't seem to fathom their relationship ended years ago."

"Ended rather abruptly."

"Yes. Maybe that's what's wrong. I don't even know, but I'll figure it out."

"Don't let him mess you up again. No one's worth that."

She smiled sadly. Why couldn't she have fallen for Hunter instead of Cameron? "Thanks, Hunter."

"All right. I'll let you go. Let me know if you need anything. Bottle of booze, a gallon of ice cream, Cam's butt in a sling."

"I appreciate it. Thanks."

When she ended the call, she didn't know if Hunter had called to ask about Cameron or to check up on her, but she was grateful for the call all the same. Debating a little, she went to get another bowl of ice cream, and turned on the TV. She'd earned it. And she didn't need new jeans right this minute anyway.

It was with a determined mindset that Skye walked to work the next day. She wasn't going to give her daddy any more reasons to call her *spacey* or tell her to go home before the workday was over. And there'd be no dessert for dinner tonight, either. At lunch, she'd call Camille and make plans for dinner. Life would get back on track, Cameron Madigan be damned.

"Morning, honey." Her daddy was enjoying a cup of coffee while going over the day's schedule when she came into the break room at the clinic.

"Good morning, Daddy." She bent down to kiss his cheek and went to hang her coat. "I thought I'd beat you here this morning. It's high time we got the Christmas decorations out, and I thought I'd start before the first patients get here."

"Ah, yes. Your momma's already going overboard at home. I've given up hoping she'll one day realize she doesn't need to buy new decorations every single year when she never throws any of the old out."

Skye smiled. "Momma loves Christmas."

As her daddy opened the morning newspaper, she figured he was probably here early because her momma was decorating. He was good at getting out of the way when holiday decorations were brought out. Well, tough. She was getting the clinic's Christmas stuff out of the storage room right now, and if he wanted to flee, he could go into his office. She'd leave that for last.

Decorating between patients, Skye had a busy day that kept her — mostly — from thinking about Cameron. She'd only caught herself daydreaming four or five times, which she considered a success. What was more important, her daddy hadn't caught her daydreaming once, and she'd made plans for dinner with Camille, so there'd be no wallowing in brownies on the couch again.

The Christmas tree in the waiting room was lit when Skye left the clinic that night. It was visible through the window, and she stood outside for a moment taking in the sight. Like her momma, she loved Christmas, and she was proud of herself for having spent some enjoyable hours decorating. In some ways, Cameron was everything. Had been when they were together and was now.

He was the only man she'd ever loved, the only one she'd ever truly wanted, and certainly the only one she'd ever felt like she needed. Once, he'd been basically her whole her life, but she refused to give him that power again.

Satisfied that she was coping and on the right path toward regaining the part of herself she'd lost once again the other night, she set her course toward the little Italian place where she was meeting Camille. Just because she felt in control of the situation didn't mean that she couldn't trash Cameron to her best friend. Just a little.

# Chapter Twelve

Money had been tight for years and spent on more essential things than alcohol, so when Cameron woke up with a massive hangover, it was an unfamiliar feeling. Though, not so unfamiliar that he had any problems identifying his condition. Death, he remembered, was the only immediate cure. Time would fix him, as well, but that would take a while. What might cure the crick in the neck he'd gotten from sleeping all night on the couch in his daddy's office was a different question entirely.

Sitting up slowly, he tried to breathe deeply as the room and his stomach spun at the same time in different directions. The empty beer bottles and the nearly empty whiskey bottle told him why. He left the office, desperate for some aspirin, coffee, and a shower in whatever order he could find them. He found the aspirin and the coffee first. Unfortunately they came with a side of Strawberry.

"I really think we should talk about your alcohol consumption, big brother. It's not safe to go to work with a hangover. Lots of dangerous tools out there, you know, and heavy machinery."

"Fuck off, kid."

"Not so fun when you're on the receiving end, huh?" Straw brought his coffee with him, and less than a minute later loud rock music shook the house in general and Cameron's brain in particular. Fucking Strawberry.

Seeking refuge in the shower, Cameron wondered what to do with his day. It was tempting to crawl into bed and hope to sleep until he was a human being again. Only then he'd have Hunter breathing down his neck for missing work. Ugh, work. Loud saws, cheerful people getting ready for the Christmas markets. However, since it didn't appear Straw was on his way to work, home meant loud, crappy music. Cameron preferred the saws.

It was past nine by the time he made it to the mill. He ignored Hunter's raised eyebrows, Reid's grin, and all the extra people they'd hired who were setting up booths, hanging strings of Christmas lights, and cleaning out a year of debris from what they called the courtyard. While he was considering the least loud, and therefor least painful, job, Hunter came over.

"Good to see you up and about. Straw coming, too?"

Cameron shrugged. "No idea. He's busy pestering the neighbors with that noise he calls music."

"It's only a question of time before someone from the county Sheriff's office stops by to talk to him. But better them than me." Hunter rolled his shoulders. "I just loaded one of the trucks with the decorations for the lane. You remember, right? If you want to set them up, go ahead. Probably less noise up there on your own."

So Straw was a shitty brother. But what did that matter when Hunter was pretty damn fantastic? "Thanks," Cameron said.

"No sweat. Catch you later."

Grateful, although he still felt as if a platoon of very small road construction workers were inside his skull, he headed for the truck and drove up the lane. It was better to start in the other end where the noise from the mill couldn't be heard. Hopefully by the time he'd placed all the decorations and gotten back, his head would feel better.

Strings of lights for the different kinds of trees lining the lane were straight forward enough. Then in between, there would be lit figures—reindeer, candy canes, santas, angels. Some of them were old and made Cameron smile as he placed them, others were new like the polar bears and the owl in the Santa hat. Very Christmassy, he thought wryly.

Several times he had to go back and load the truck again, but in general the lonesome, silent task suited him just fine. It was inevitable that his thoughts strayed to Skye.

She'd hit him right where it hurt the most. It wasn't his pride that had taken the biggest blow, however. It was his heart. With the combined hit, he was nearly proud of himself for not being rolled up in the fetal position somewhere.

To be sure, he hadn't seen it coming although he'd been afraid of someone finding out. And, in the harsh light of day, he could hardly blame her for not wanting to be involved with someone who'd already hurt her once and who was living a lie. If there had been something he could do to change it, he would have. But no matter what he did, a glorious Nashville career wasn't going to materialize out of thin air, nor would his lie go away.

It hadn't even been a lie at first. He'd just let people think what they wanted—what he wanted—and from there it had escalated. And once people found out the truth, and they would because if Skye could find out, so could everyone else, he'd be laughed out of town. If not because he hadn't made it big, then definitely because he'd tried to hide the truth. "Be a man," had been one of his daddy's favorite phrases, but Cameron was fully aware that he'd never listened.

By lunchtime, he'd only finished about a fourth of the long lane. It took longer than he'd expected to string the lights. Since the thought of food had made him dry heave when he'd left the house, he hadn't brought his usual sandwiches. So he kept on working.

Hunter came to the rescue again. On one of the ATVs, he came up the lane at the same time as Straw zoomed down it in his beat-up truck. For one terrifying moment, Cameron was sure they'd collide as the lane had plenty of curves, but at the last second Hunter pulled in between the trees. When he reached Cameron, he looked as steamed as Cameron felt.

"That fucking Strawberry!"

"I'm gonna kill him," Cameron swore. "Slow and painfully."

Hunter blew out a breath. "We gotta do something about that kid. Talking doesn't help. Wanna help me beat him up? Killing him can come later."

"If I thought it would help, I'd have clocked him long ago. But you're right. We need to do something, but I really don't know what."

"Me neither." Hunter shook his head and handed over a paper bag and a thermos. "Lunch."

"Thanks." Cameron studied his brother. "Why are you so nice to me today?"

"I try not to kick someone who's already down."

*Ouch.* Cameron winced. He wasn't sure he liked being so transparent. There were always things inside it was best if no one saw.

\* \* \* \*

She was being a coward. She knew it when she dialed her brother, she knew it when she asked if he had plans for the weekend, and she definitely knew it when she started looking at alternative destinations for a weekend away after Sebastian ruefully told her about his double shift at the hospital. But Skye didn't care. If she wanted to stick her head in the sand, she would. It wasn't that unusual for her to take a weekend away somewhere to relax, write, or just to see some different people and some different places.

The irony wasn't lost on her when she found herself in Nashville late Friday evening. She hadn't told André she was flying in, or he'd be dragging her around to meet people all weekend. That wasn't why she'd decided to come to Nashville. No, she wanted to get lost in the crowd, to listen to music, and to remind herself that she was more than just a woman pining for a man who wasn't good for her. She was one of the leading songwriters in a business who didn't know who she was, and it was time to get a real taste of what that meant.

She attended a couple of concerts with artists she'd written songs for, she stayed out late getting tipsy and let the atmosphere and the soul of the city absorb into her memory.

She'd been there before, of course, but it was nice to be reminded. And this time she knew she wouldn't accidentally run into Cameron, which made her relax.

Of course, being alone in Nashville made her think too closely about what had transpired with Cameron. She was having a cup of coffee Sunday morning before heading home, thoughts floating randomly around in her head, when she realized that she'd been unfair to accuse Cameron of lying. She had lied, too.

It wasn't the same exactly, but was it really worse to lie about your failure than it was to lie about your success? Skye put down her coffee cup. The chatter around her faded until she was stuck in a vacuum. Lord, she'd been unfair and rude. Full of double standards. It wasn't even any consolation that Cameron didn't know — somehow that just made it worse.

She could admit the truth to him, of course, but what did she really owe him that she didn't owe everyone else? Her parents knew she wrote music, occasionally making a buck or two, but they didn't know the particulars. Camille knew, too, but again Skye had shared no details, and Camille hadn't asked. And why was that? Skye finished her coffee as she pondered it. Respect and not wanting to pry was probably why Camille hadn't asked. She had plenty of secrets and hidden sides to her own personality, and Skye respected that.

As for why Skye hadn't told the people closest to her exactly what she did, how well she did it, and how often her words could be heard on the radio, she admitted to herself that Cameron's failure had probably scared her so much that she'd rather keep things general and vague than go into detail about every success and every failure.

Which was cowardly. But it was what it was. Like Cameron couldn't change the charade he'd kept up for years, she couldn't change how she'd handled things either. More so, she didn't want to. The anonymity was too precious to her.

She did a little shopping on the way back to the hotel. It was good for the soul. A new jacket that she didn't know how she'd managed to live without for so long, a gorgeous purse she'd give Camille for Christmas, and a new pipe for her daddy. A little music store caught her eye, and she spent an hour picking out old classics for herself and those she knew would appreciate them. In the Ms, she sighed when she saw Cameron's first and only album priced at ninety-nine cents.

A man's big dreams reduced to less than a dollar. Her heart broke a little in her chest, and she hoped he'd never seen what would have been his pride and joy on sale. She put it into her pile although she already had a copy at home, unlike pretty much everyone else in the world. The album had been, in the unforgettable words of André who'd told her years ago, an epic failure.

On her laptop, Skye listened to the album on the plane home. Although she'd bought it as soon as she'd found out it had been released, she hadn't listened to it much. She'd made a point not to, in fact, at first afraid it would shatter the fragile control she'd regained over her heart. As the music and Cameron's voice washed over her through the ear buds, she wondered how the people who'd spotted him had made him release such sloppy work.

There was nothing wrong with his voice. It was smooth as whiskey, but with a smoky twist that made it interesting. She'd listened to him sing so many times, and it still gave her chill bumps. The songs he sang, however, were sloppily written and not the stuff that made a career. He hadn't had a chance because the one he'd been given hadn't been sincere.

Had she given him a chance?

* * * *

Cameron was all Christmassed out when he got home. Through the weekend, he'd decorated and strung lights until his brain had turned numb. And made him dumb.

But at least now they'd run out of decorations, and he'd return to normal duties tomorrow morning. He missed the big circular saw.

"Who's cooking?" he asked Reid when he came downstairs after a hot shower.

"Straw." Reid was on his laptop at the kitchen table. "But he isn't here."

"Great." Cameron grabbed a bottle of water from the fridge and peered into the dishwasher. Full. He turned it on and considered it his domestic duty of the day.

Hunter came in. "Whose turn is it to cook?"

"Straw's," Reid and Cameron said in unison.

"But he isn't here," Reid added.

"Fucking Strawberry. He left work before any of us, and that's after not showing up until after lunch. Again."

"Kid's a nightmare." Reid reached for the takeout menu from the only place in Maeville that delivered. "Wanna order some pizzas? I'm not cooking just because Straw's out getting wasted. Again."

So they ordered pizzas and ate them in almost complete silence. Reid was still on the laptop, and Hunter was reading the newspaper. Cameron ate his large pepperoni while wondering how long he and Skye could keep avoiding each other in a town the size of Maeville. He hadn't seen her since he'd left her cabin with his heart in tatters. Until he figured out what to say to her, it was probably for the best.

Hunter folded the paper. "What are we gonna do about Straw? If this keeps up, I'm seriously afraid one of us will have to bail him out of jail or ID him down at the county morgue before long."

Cameron was fresh out of ideas about what to do, but he'd passed annoyance and was also scared of what would happen if things continued as they had. Talking to him had been a fiasco.

Reid had a suggestion, though. "Let's hogtie him when he comes back and haul him onto my boat. A couple of weeks on the water without land in sight might make a man out of him. Plus, no access to whatever he's polluting his system with."

"It's not a bad idea," Hunter said. "Except you guys can't go away for a couple of weeks and still meet the requirements of Daddy's will."

"Crap. I can try taking him out for a couple of days, though. Might make a difference that he can't just leave when he doesn't like what's being said."

"Or he might murder you in your sleep or throw you overboard," Cameron said flatly. The drinking was bad enough, but he was fed up with Straw's childish behavior. He wasn't a teenager rebelling against the old man anymore. He was an adult who needed to learn how to take responsibility for his own life. And suppose you took your own advice, Cameron taunted himself in his head.

"There is that," Reid reluctantly agreed. "We could make house rules, but no one's interested in scaring him off and ruining it for everyone."

"Y'all think he'd respond well to added responsibility?" Hunter asked and sipped his beer before continuing. "He's mad about being called a kid, being called Strawberry, and he's mad about being the youngest, the one who didn't get a chance to be something, mad about every fucking thing. So maybe if we treat him like an adult, he starts acting like one?"

Reid frowned. "What, you want us to call him Julian? We tried that when he was eleven or twelve, remember? Then he decided Straw was better than Jules."

That made them all chuckle despite the serious topic. Shortening his name had gotten him over his Call-Me-Julian period pretty quickly.

"And what do you have in mind for added responsibility? We can't let him fuck up the mill." Cameron used to hate the place as much as Straw seemed to do now, but he saw it—along with a lot of other things—differently now. He felt possessive of the mill, of their legacy. Not because he'd suddenly forgiven his daddy, but generations of Madigans before them had put blood, sweat, and tears into that mill. One screwed up runt wasn't going to ruin it.

"Call him whatever you want," Hunter replied. "Well, except Jules. And I don't have anything specific in mind. Maybe we all need to sit down and talk about how to divide the jobs. We all have aspects of the mill we like and dislike, so we might as well iron out who does what. Not just for Straw's sake, but for everyone's. And for the mill's. There's no reason we shouldn't play to our strengths."

"That's a good point," Cameron admitted.

"Yeah, it is," Reid agreed. "I hate it when you're so smart. Makes the rest of us look like dolts."

"Well, that part's not hard." Hunter chuckled and ducked when Cameron and Reid both swung at him.

"So we all sit down and talk." Reid rose and started—voluntarily, which made Cameron suspect he was coming down with something—clearing the table for pizza boxes and empty cans and bottles.

"As soon as he comes back," Hunter agreed. Then hesitated. "Well maybe it's better tomorrow. There's no telling which state he'll return in, or how late."

"Tomorrow." Cameron rose, too, and headed for the living room and the TV. He felt hopeful that they'd finally come up with something that would work.

Except, the following morning there was no Straw. His truck wasn't parked outside, and none of the others had heard him come or go. The day passed with no sign of him, as did the following night. Just when they'd thought they had a solution to the Strawberry problem, he'd up and disappeared.

"Fucking Strawberry," Cameron muttered to himself as he went to bed that second night, but there was no anger or annoyance inside of him. Just fear.

# Chapter Thirteen

"Maeville Medical Clinic, how may I help you?" Skye held the phone between her ear and her shoulder while rearranging the folders and the brochures on the rack on the wall. It had been a slow day.

"Hey, it's me," Camille's voice sounded in her ear. "You haven't seen Julian in the past few days, have you?"

"No, I haven't." Skye hadn't seen any of the Madigans since before she'd gone to Nashville, which was most likely because she'd limited her social interactions to those required by the clinic. She'd even neglected Camille and her parents. "Why? Is something wrong?"

"I hope not," Camille replied, but her tone told Skye that she was really worried. "It's just that no one's seen him since Sunday afternoon. He's taken off for days, even weeks, before, but not since Mr. Madigan died."

"Do they think something's happened, or that he's just decided that he doesn't want to go along with what was in the will?"

"I don't think they know what to think. He didn't say anything to anyone before disappearing. I was probably the last one who saw him before he left. He blew me off when I asked about an order and then drove off like a bat out of hell. But that's not new. He always blows people off and drives like a maniac."

Skye thought back to when she'd found him by the side of the road outside town. "Have they looked for him?"

"In town, yeah. Reid was told at the county Sheriff's office that they've got no reason to think he hasn't just gone off on a bender or something. Hunter just drove up river to look for him. Julian's been fishing up near the outlet on and off for years."

"I'll keep an eye out," Skye promised. "If there's anything I can do, let me know."

"Ask around maybe? You see a lot of people every day."

"You bet. Keep in touch."

Skye hung up with a frown. Demons haunted Julian Madigan, and she dearly hoped they hadn't gotten a hold of him. She marched into her daddy's office. "Daddy?"

He put down the medical journal he was reading, taking advantage of the slow day. "Yes, honey?"

"Camille just called. No one's seen Julian since Sunday. Can you handle things here alone?"

"Yes, of course, but what are you going to do?"

"Go look for him. Remember a couple of weeks ago, I found him drunk outside town? I don't know, but I'll feel better if I do something. And it's not like we're busy."

"That's true," her daddy allowed. "Do you want me to close up and come with you?"

She smiled. "No thanks, but I appreciate the offer. If you get any patients, can you ask them if they've seen Julian? I promised Camille."

"I'll ask. Be safe, Skye."

Nodding, she went to change out of her scrubs and then hurried home to get her car. She didn't really think she'd find him by the side of the road again, but going out to look would make her feel better than just sitting at the empty clinic.

He wasn't there, of course, nor anywhere else on that stretch of road. After driving around aimlessly for a while, she parked and went down to the river. She'd always been able to find peace down there, just like she knew Cameron did. If Julian knew where to find peace, she didn't know, but she truly believed peace was what he needed.

She hadn't really expected him to find down by the river, either. He'd been gone for days, and it was cold outside. Unless he'd been hurt, and she refused to think that way, he'd be holed up somewhere inside where it was warm. Most likely he'd be drunk or high, but as long as he was safe, it would be okay. She shuddered and buried her hands in her pockets. She couldn't imagine what Cameron, Hunter, and Reid might be feeling. How they'd cope if something had happened to Julian, or how furious they'd be when he strolled back into the house after a bender.

Skye jumped a mile when she heard a voice up ahead. For a moment, she thought she'd found Julian, but then she saw Cameron through the trees. He was hauling rocks into the water and yelling…at Julian apparently.

"Fucking, stupid kid!" He flung another rock. "You're the most inconsiderate, childish little bastard. Not a lick better than Daddy. Shit."

Skye looked around. Cameron was most definitely alone and letting out some steam. She was just considering turning back when he spotted her, letting a rock fall from his hand instead of throwing it in the water. "Skye."

"Hi."

"I was just…" He pulled his gloves off only to put them back on. "Straw's missing."

"Yeah, I know. Camille called. I thought I'd come out and look for him, too."

"Really? I mean…crap. Thanks." Cameron sighed. "The little shit's done nothing but annoy me since I came back, and now I'm going out of my mind worrying about him."

"Sounds like typical brothers."

That made him smile. "Yeah, I guess so."

Skye didn't trust herself with him anymore. The strong hold on herself and her heart she thought she'd regained was nothing but an illusion. Now that he was standing right there she had to force herself not to jump into his arms and stay there until the end of time. She swallowed with some difficulty. Be strong, she told herself. "I'll just head back the other way again. See you."

* * * *

"Skye, wait." The words were out of his mouth before he'd thought through why he wanted her to stay. He was as needy for her as he was needy for his next breath of air. It sounded melodramatic even in his head, but it felt true nonetheless.

"Listen, I…" He took a deep breath and plunged ahead although he hadn't planned to. "I'm sorry. You're right, I've been lying about my career, or rather the lack of a career, all along. I failed miserably. It's been years since I've sung or stood on a stage. Every music-related dream I've ever had has been ground into dust, but you have to understand that I didn't set out to lie. Not to you, not to anybody.

"But…I know it's not an excuse, but it was easier to let people think what they wanted than to correct them and admit I was a failure."

When he stopped to take another deep breath, he braved a look at Skye. She stood calmly and looked at him as if he'd just told her it was cold out today, and not that he was the most epic fiasco to make it out of Nashville in decades. Okay, maybe that was stretching it, but it was what it felt like when no one—as in absolutely no one—had turned up to the last gig he'd been booked for. And when he'd been laughed at when he'd asked if he'd still get paid.

"I know, Cam, and I know you don't want my sympathy, but I'm sorry. Sorry it happened to you and sorry you felt like you had to lie about it."

He swallowed. "How do you know?"

"I've known almost all along. A friend told me."

"A friend…" Cameron imagined in his head the whole town knew and were just humoring him by letting him pretend he was a star. He felt sick. "Who else knows?"

She shook her head. "I don't know. I haven't told anyone, and the friend who told me isn't from around here. He just knew we had history."

Whoever this friend was, Cameron decided he didn't like him. Loathed him, in fact. The anger rose inside of him alongside the humiliation. "And I'm to believe you knew all this time and told no one? Not even Camille? Or Hunter?"

"I didn't tell anyone, Cam."

"Why not? I'd screwed you over."

Skye smiled sadly. "That's why I kept it to myself. Because I know what being screwed over feels like. I didn't deserve it from you, and you didn't deserve it from the people who were supposed to help you in Nashville. I kept quiet for your sake."

He paced between the trees. There wasn't a lot of room, so it was very unsatisfactory, but he needed to move and get rid of some of the nervous energy. "At first, I kept thinking to myself that you'd come, too. We'd always talked about it."

"You thought I'd come running after you'd left me? That's either an extremely naïve or an extremely self-centered way of thinking."

"I know. Some days I hoped you'd come anyway. Other days I was afraid you would. Afraid you'd show up and expose me. You could have come and ignored the hell out of me while going after your dream. Why didn't you? The songs you wrote back then, Skye…they'd blow the socks off most of the stuff that's being released today. Imagine if you hadn't given up on your dream."

"Imagine if you hadn't given up on ours." She shuffled uncomfortably. "I'm not saying this to be nasty, and before you point it out, I know I've been lying as much as you have. But I didn't give up on my dream. I'm living it."

He only just held back the sneer. "I don't mean nursing."

"Neither do I. I partnered up with André O'Hare five years ago. My dream's become reality."

Cameron stared. If she'd hit him with a sledgehammer, he wouldn't have recovered faster. "André O'Hare. Blue Skies. For real?"

She nodded.

Everyone in Nashville knew who André O'Hare was. No one knew who his partner, Blue Skies, was. But it was common knowledge that if you went to them—and weren't turned away—you'd be getting a hit.

A wave of conflicting emotions coursed through Cameron. Pride because he knew how difficult it was to actually make it in the business. Regret that he hadn't known and that he'd cast aside his chance of being a part of it. Anger at fate for his fiasco lined up against her success. Embarrassment that he didn't measure up in any way to the woman he loved. And weariness about the whole thing.

"Mind blown," he said. He didn't know what else to say, but then he remembered himself. "Congratulations. I promised myself years ago not to willingly listen to music, but I've been forced to listen at the places I've worked since then, and it's impossible not to know what you've been up to. Wow."

"I didn't tell you to gloat. You expect me to tell no one about you, and I expect the same of you."

"Why the hell aren't you shouting it from the rooftops? You're a success!" It was a mystery to him, but hell, so was Skye. Women in general, but Skye in particular.

"I'm a success whether or not I shout it from the rooftops. Success isn't defined by how many people know. I know, which is what matters. The singers who sing my songs and the people who listen to them are happy either way."

"I won't tell." He wanted to, but he knew he was getting a good deal with her promising not to tell anyone about his failure. "Does no one know?"

"You know," she replied with a small smile. She didn't look the least bit comfortable, which he should have remembered. She'd never wanted the spotlight. "Camille knows some, as do my parents. And André. That's it."

Nope. He didn't get it.

* * * *

It was like an agreement of mutual destruction, Skye reflected as she walked back toward her car. Though, destruction was probably not the right word.

Cameron wouldn't be destroyed if people found out he hadn't accomplished what he'd set out to, just as she wouldn't be destroyed if people learned what she did in her spare time. Life as they knew — and preferred — it would just be a thing of the past. Neither wanted that, so she was confident their secrets would be kept. It just didn't get them anywhere. They were still stuck in limbo.

She drove around looking for Julian, but she knew he wasn't an idiot. If he wanted to stay lost, he could. And would. The forest that fed the mill surrounded Maeville, and in it there were lots of hunting cabins where someone could hide out. And Julian knew the forest like the back of his hand.

When she came home, Camille was waiting for her outside.

"What are you doing out here? It's freezing, and you've got a key."

"For emergencies," Camille pointed out. "This wasn't one. I just got here like two minutes ago."

Sky shook her head. Even if Camille had been waiting for an hour, she wouldn't have used the key.

They cooked together and then shared a bottle of wine while eating pasta and discussing what might have happened to Julian.

"I think he's hiding," Camille said. "He must be."

Skye nodded, although she thought it was a very real possibility that he'd gotten himself in trouble after drinking too much.

"I went out to some of the closest cabins on Madigan land, but they looked as if they haven't been used in decades. Hunter went up river, but his fishing buddies up there said they haven't seen him in weeks." Camille sipped her wine. "Reid and Cam went to talk to those motorcycle gang guys Julian hangs out with sometimes, but they wouldn't say a thing. And the Sheriff won't lift a finger."

"I went out looking for him, too. Outside town and down by the river. I ran into Cam, which distracted me for a while." Skye topped off their wine glasses. "If it's not one Madigan frustrating the hell out of me, it's another. Why can't they all be more like Hunter?"

"They are," Camille replied dryly. "Hunter's as frustrating as the rest of them."

"Why do we like them again?"

"Because on the rare occasions they're not frustrating, they're pretty damn amazing."

"Right." Skye nodded. Sarcasm aside, Camille was right. Perhaps Reid and Cameron had been as lost as Julian was right now, but when they'd needed to stand together, they had. At least for a while. "Okay, stupid question, but have they tried calling his phone?"

"Yep. And if he's checking his voicemail, he might stay away for good. I've overheard some of the tirades they've delivered. They're not happy, and even their worry comes out as anger."

"Men."

After they'd eaten, they made quick work of the dishes and had just put on an old black and white movie to watch when Camille's cell phone rang.

"It's Julian." Giddy laughter escaped her when she checked the caller ID. Accepting the call, she switched to speakerphone and put the phone down on the coffee table. "Julian?"

"Hey."

"Oh my heavens, am I happy to hear your voice. Are you okay?"

"Yeah, I'm..." He cleared his throat and fell silent.

Skye and Camille looked at each other. "Honey, where are you?" Camille asked gently. "We've been so worried."

"Greenville." Once again, he cleared his throat. "Can you maybe come pick me up? I don't know who else to ask. I don't want my brothers to know."

Camille rose immediately. "Of course. I'm bringing Skye, though. I don't like driving outside town in the dark. Where are you exactly?"

"'Kay. Thanks. I'm at the Vidant Medical Center. I don't know the address, but it's where we picked up Daddy last year when he had that knee surgery."

"I remember, and I'm on my way. Just tell me one thing. Are you hurt?"

"I'll be okay. See ya."

"Stupid boy is definitely hurt." Camille pocketed her phone. "You'll come with me, won't you? I'd ask Hunter, but imagine being trapped in a car with the two of them for an hour and a half."

"Try and stop me. I wonder what he's done to himself. Hospital…" Skye shook her head and blew out the candles before going out to grab her coat and purse. Mentally, she was waving goodbye to the good night's sleep she'd been counting on. Greenville was a hundred and sixty miles round trip, and this time she wasn't just going to dump Julian on the Madigans' front porch. If he was really hurt, the last thing he needed was to be left alone with three angry brothers. Even if he might have done something stupid.

They talked very little on the way to Greenville. Theories floated around in Skye's mind, though, getting more and more dramatic the closer they got to actually finding out. Julian's car was missing, but since he apparently couldn't get home on his own, the natural thing to assume that he was in hospital because he'd crashed it. Either that, or he was too hurt to do any driving on his own.

"His brothers are going to kill him if he's gotten hurt because of his own stupidity," Camille said. "Oh lord, does this stretch of road seem longer than usual to you, too?"

"Yeah." Skye felt as if they should be nearing the West Coast instead of Greenville. She jumped in her seat when her phone rang.

"Is it Julian?" Camille asked.

Skye checked the screen. "No, it's Cam. Damn. If I answer it, I have to lie to him. If I don't, he's probably going to keep calling."

"Lie."

Skye shrugged. It wouldn't be the first time. "Hey, Cam."

# Chapter Fourteen

Cameron forgot he had no reason for calling Skye when he picked up on the fact that she wasn't at home. It sounded like she was in a car. An old car, which ruled out her own. She'd already exhausted him emotionally today, but now jealousy reared its ugly head, even though he had absolutely no right to be jealous if she was taking an evening drive with some guy in an old, crappy car. From the window, he could see his own old, crappy car and cursed, not for the first time, that he couldn't afford a new one.

"Cam?"

"Yeah. Um, hi. I just wanted to…well, are you busy?"

She hesitated. "Kind of. Can I call you back tomorrow or is it important?"

"Nope, not important at all. Absolutely not." *Go on back to your cheap date*, he thought. "I just wanted to check in in case you'd heard from Straw."

"Sorry, I haven't. I'll let you know when or if I do."

"Right. Goodnight then."

"Goodnight, Cam."

He stared at his phone. That, too, was old and crappy. Most things he owned were. Of course, getting new ones wouldn't make him a better or happier man. Not when the woman he loved was in someone else's car at—he checked his watch—ten-thirty in the evening. What had possessed him to call her so late anyway? It was his own damn fault that his mood was even worse now.

"Cam?" Hunter pushed the door open. "I saw the light on. You busy?"

"Nope."

Hunter looked like hell. He was taking Straw's disappearance the hardest and spent nearly every waking hour either working or looking for the kid. Reid and Cameron were better at pacing themselves, plus much more inclined to believe that Straw was just fucking with them. At least some of the time, Cameron admitted to himself.

"I'll head over to the Sheriff's in the morning. Nag them, beg them, threaten them, I don't know. But they've got to do something. I just searched Straw's room again, and I found weed and some pills. I have no idea what those are, but they were in a plastic baggie, not in a prescription bottle. What if he owes someone more money than he has?"

"Then he's a bigger idiot than I thought."

"I'm serious." Hunter yanked a frustrated hand through his hair. He looked exhausted. Old even.

"So am I. We'll have to start calling you 'Momma' soon the way you carry on with your worrying."

"Jesus Christ, why do I even try?"

Hunter walked out, shoulders slumped and posture resigned. Cameron felt a little bad, but he was sick and tired of having Straw dictate his life. The little shit wasn't even around, and still they all danced after his pipe like they did when he was there, playing his stupid music, having his tantrums, and blowing off work whenever he felt like it and left others to pick up the slack. The only reason Cameron wanted him to come back was so they could have their inheritance. He sighed. And that was a lie. He was worried about Straw, too, but he was going to strangle him if it turned out he'd just been getting drunk or high.

Hours later, he was fast asleep when he was torn from a dream where he was surrounded by old cars driven by dark-haired beauties with green eyes. There had been hundreds of them. He stared into the darkness. Then heard the doorbell. The glowing numbers on the alarm clock suggested to his bleary eyes that it was nearly two in the morning.

Groaning, he got out of bed, not bothering to put anything on except the boxer shorts he already wore. As he stumbled down the stairs, the bell sounded again, and both Hunter and Reid stuck out their heads from their respective rooms.

"Who is it?" Reid asked.

"How the hell should I know?" Cameron nearly nose-dived from the middle of staircase, but managed to grab hold of the banister. "Fuck."

Turning on the lights as he went, he finally made it to the front door, which he wrenched open. Skye and Camille stood outside, disgustingly bright-eyed and beautiful. But then, when weren't they? The porch light reflected in Skye's hair made him want to write a song. But then he remembered he was standing across from Blue Skies. Maybe not.

"Ladies?" he drawled, too tired to think of just one good reason for why they were there.

"Nice form there, boss," Camille said. Her eyes slid up to meet his, making it obvious where they'd been. She was biting her lip, trying not to grin. She wasn't succeeding very well.

"Come around this time of night, sugar, and you'll have to take what you get." He stepped aside. "Want to come in for a glass of sweet tea? I'm sure there's more of that Hummingbird cake Reid whipped up earlier. Grandma's recipe is a winner every time."

"You can cut the sarcasm, *sugar*," Skye told him dryly. "We know it's the middle of the night, but we've got a present for you that needs immediate delivery. It's in the car. You'll have to go and get it yourself."

"Good thing I'm dressed for it." Cameron shivered as he stepped into Reid's sneakers by the door and went outside in the freezing night air. What men didn't do to humor women.

Hoping none of the neighbors were up and looking out their windows, Cameron had almost made it to the car when he realized that he could at least have put on a jacket. Then he spotted the side of Straw's face pressed against the car window, a white bandage on his forehead and discolored skin around it. Relief like he couldn't remember ever feeling before made the breath whoosh out of his body. Stupid kid.

"He's drugged up," Skye said right behind him. "Prescription drugs."

"You better be staying for that sweet tea. I want the full story," Cameron warned her and opened the car door. With some difficulty, he managed to drag an unconscious Straw inside, where, with Hunter's help, he was parked on the nearest couch.

Reid handed Cameron a pair of sweats and a t-shirt and announced to the girls that the show was over. Cameron rolled his eyes but put on the clothes.

Hunter made tea like the good momma he was, and before long Cameron and his two brothers were seated in the living room looking at Skye and Camille, who had yet to explain how and where they'd found Straw.

"Well?" Cameron prompted them.

"Just don't fire me," Camille begged.

"Not even if you've kicked Straw's ass yourself," Cameron promised. "In fact, that would actually earn you a bonus."

\* \* \* \*

It was probably due to lack of sleep, but the very idea of Camille kicking Julian's ass made Skye smother a giggle. She felt Cameron's eyes on her, but she didn't meet his gaze.

"Julian called me earlier from Greenville and asked me for a lift. He didn't want you guys to know, although I have no idea why since he asked to be driven home." Camille gnawed at her lip and fidgeted with her hands in her lap. Skye wasn't sure why. The Madigans knew every well they couldn't get by without Camille, so fearing for her job was silly.

"When we got there," Camille continued, "he was waiting outside. He just said he'd been in an accident and that his car was toast. We stopped by the pharmacy to get his prescription filled, and soon after he'd taken a couple of the pills, he conked out."

"So we stopped by the police station in Greenville and asked about the accident," Skye continued when it was clear that Camille wasn't going to share that little detail. Of course, the fact that she'd told the officer that she was Julian's sister-in-law to get any information out of him wasn't something she was going to share, either. Camille didn't even know as she'd been on Julian Watch. "It was a solo accident. He hit a tree, totaled his car, and has been in hospital since Sunday."

"What, unconscious?" Hunter asked.

"No," Skye replied. "I know what you're asking, and yes, it was his choice not to contact anyone."

When no one said anything, she cleared her throat and continued, "I asked if he'd been charged with DWI, but the police said his blood alcohol level wasn't over the limit."

"For once." Cameron got up to pace. "So, how bad is the moron hurt?"

"Concussion, lots of cuts and bruises. They were worried about internal bleeding, which was why they kept him so long for observation, but he's been cleared. The police had checked up on his condition." Skye rose and took her own and Camille's untouched cups, heading for the kitchen. "We'll go now."

She rinsed the cups and put them in the sink. The long day and the even longer night were catching up with her, and she couldn't wait to get home and fall into blessed sleep. Returning to the living room, Camille was waiting for her by the door.

"Thanks for bringing him home," Hunter told them.

"You're welcome," Camille replied. "Goodnight."

Halfway to the car, Cameron caught up with them and put a hand on Skye's arm to make her stop. "Thanks. I'm...I'm sorry about earlier."

"Nothing to be sorry for." She gave him the best attempt at a smile she could muster. "Goodnight, Cam."

She blew out a breath when they were inside the car. When she turned her head, she could still see Cameron's silhouette in the front yard. She waved halfheartedly.

"That went…well," Camille commented as she started the car.

"You think?" Skye laughed tiredly. "God, what a night. I hope they're not too rough on poor Julian tomorrow."

"He should have called them to let them know where he was. That he was okay. Well, relatively okay."

They hadn't talked much on the way home from Greenville, not wanting Julian to wake up and overhear them talking about him.

"Yeah, he should have. Maybe he just didn't think they'd care."

"Bullshit. They may do little else but work against each other, but if they doubt the love that binds them together, they're bigger idiots than I thought." Camille turned down the lane toward Skye's cabin. "They don't know how lucky they are to have each other."

Skye reached over and squeezed Camille's arm. "Blood's not everything. They don't know how lucky they are to have you, but I know exactly how lucky I am. Drive safely home. Goodnight, sweetie."

Camille smiled at her, looking like a tired angel in the unforgiving light in the car when Skye opened the door. "Thanks. I needed that. Goodnight."

Skye watched her drive off, and then dragged herself inside. It took her just a few minutes before she was lying in her bed and waiting for sleep to claim her. But of course it didn't. Her tired mind brought up images of Cameron when he'd opened the door, looking much too sexy to display himself like that to just anyone.

Lord. She groaned and turned over. It was clear they'd woken him up, but it was as if he'd dressed, or, well, undressed, for the occasion just to torture her. It was almost three in the morning, and if she didn't get some sleep very— *very*— soon, the clinic's patients would need a doctor just for having dealt with the grouchy nurse.

A night without much sleep like the one she'd shared with Cameron not that long ago, but one without the benefits he'd added was just asking for a bad day to follow it.

Tossing and turning, fighting to get Cameron out of her mind, it was more than an hour later when she finally nodded off. Seconds after remembering it was her birthday. What a way to start the day.

* * * *

The first thing Cameron did the next morning was make coffee. When he'd made one pot, he poured it into a couple of thermoses and started a second pot. He figured a pot each would suffice, at least to start out with. He didn't know whether or not to include Straw in that. Having your coffee made for you was something you earned in the Madigan household, and there were a lot of things Cameron could think of that Straw deserved, but coffee wasn't one of them.

Normally, he would have grabbed the easiest thing around for breakfast and hurried out the door before everyone else descended and caused general mayhem, arguing about who did what, why, and why not. It was an unspoken rule in the house that no one did anything before they'd griped about it, even if it was just turning on the coffee or taking out the trash.

Which Hunter hadn't done the night before, Cameron noted when he checked. But because he had no intentions of going to work before he'd gotten an explanation out of Straw, and therefore probably had all the time in the world, Cameron decided to cook a proper breakfast. If someone had gone grocery shopping lately, that was.

Hunter was the first to stumble in, offering a nod and a grunt in lieu of good morning before heading straight for the coffee.

Limited by the content of the refrigerator, Cameron was making bacon, toast and scrambled eggs. Though, whoever came down last was likely to miss out on the bacon as there hadn't been much left. He slid a plate across the table to Hunter and sat down himself.

"Thanks." Hunter dug in immediately. "Straw up yet?"

"No, still conked out on the couch. Figured we'd talk to him before leaving."

"You bet your ass. I've had it with that kid."

They ate in silence until Reid came down, taking the direct route to the coffee just as Cameron had expected. Reid drank greedily until he'd emptied his mug.

"I'm waking up Straw," he announced.

Cameron glanced at Hunter to see if he was going to object, but he said nothing. So they let Reid go to town. Like Hunter, he was sometimes a little hard to rile up, but when he got going, he was as bad as Cameron and Straw. They heard that when the radio in the living room was turned up to a deafening volume.

Cameron bit back a smile when he heard Straw's complaints over the cheery pop song on the radio. Then the volume was turned down, and Reid returned to the kitchen, where he filled a plate with toast, eggs, and the last of the bacon and sat down.

"Straw will be right out," he said.

Straw looked like hell. He was pale, and the bruises on his forehead stood out. Barely glancing at them, he limped past the table and grabbed a glass of water to swallow his pain medication with before going for the coffee. He ignored the toast and the eggs and sat down. "Okay, get it out. Yell, punch, lecture, whatever."

No one said anything. Cameron didn't want to give Straw what he was expecting although he'd planned to do plenty of yelling and lecturing, though perhaps he'd figured the car accident had already covered the punching part.

"All right then. See y'all later." Straw started to get up.

"No, not all right. You'll sit your ass down and not get up until someone tells you to." Hunter didn't yell, but there was no doubt he was deadly serious. Cameron had never heard his voice that cold before.

"You know, if Mr. Kane had dropped by in the past couple of days, and trust me he will be dropping by sometime, y'all would all have lost your inheritance. Not because you weren't here, Straw, but because we didn't know where you were, or if you were even coming back. And you don't get it.

"None of you gets it. Daddy didn't make out the will the way he did to punish you, or to have one final dig at you. He didn't love me anymore than he loved you, but he did know you a whole lot better than you bothered to know him. He knew if he'd just split the business in four, you'd have left me here to deal with everything and expected me to buy you guys out. To get you to stay, he had to make you. Asking wasn't enough. And Daddy wanted this family to be together. If not physically, then at least emotionally. That's what he's making us do now. And you know what, Straw? Cam put his career in Nashville on hold for this. Reid turned his back on the sea for us. And what have we given up? Nothing. So how about we start giving them, and each other, some respect, huh? I've had it with your attitude. We all have."

The silence stretched for a while until Reid rose from the table to go rinse his plate. With his back turned, he barked out a humorless laugh. "I think I know what you're doing, Straw. You did it to Daddy, and now you're doing it to us. You're testing us — do we really care about poor, little Strawberry? Well, screw you. Screw you and your self-pity. You want your inheritance, don't you?"

Straw kept staring down at his hands.

"Don't you?" Reid repeated, harsher this time as he turned around.

"Of course I fucking do," Straw bit out. "I deserve it as much as Hunter."

"Then start acting like you do. Because I can easily live without owning part of the sawmill, and if you continue acting like a dumbass, getting drunk, getting high, acting like you don't have to pull your weight, then I'm gone. Out of here. I'm just itching for a reason to leave, and you're giving me one every single day."

When Reid walked out of the kitchen, Straw turned to look at Cameron with a nonchalant look in his eyes and his nose turned up a bit too much. "I guess that just leaves you, big brother. Got something you wanna say to me, as well?"

"Yeah." Cameron's chair scraped noisily across the floor as he stood up. "Next time you need to be bailed out of trouble, leave Skye and Camille out of it. Start acting like the man your birth certificate claims you are. And one last thing. It's your turn to do the dishes."

# Chapter Fifteen

"Happy birthday, Skye."

Skye smiled. "Thank you, Harry."

There were both positive and negative things about living in a small town. Irritations and blessings. Every year, without fail, at least every other patient who came to the clinic on Skye's birthday brought her flowers, baked goodies, or little presents. If some days were long and full of demanding patients, they sure made up for it every year in December. First for her birthday and later for Christmas, where she never needed to bake cookies with all the tins and jars she and her daddy received as presents. Though, of course she baked anyway. Who could resist?

She administered the flu shot Harry had come in for and sent him on his way. Then she bounced Allison Gallagher's baby while the new momma complained about her latest rash or pain to the doctor. Allison Gallagher always had a new disease she'd read all about on the Internet.

"You going out for lunch?" her daddy asked her just after noon.

"Yeah, I thought I might. I got up late this morning, so I didn't have time to make anything to bring."

"Your momma just came over with your favorite smoked salmon sandwiches. And apple pie."

"Remind me to get her an extra big Christmas present this year." Wasting no time, Skye headed toward the break room where she greeted her momma with a hug.

"Happy birthday, honey."

"Thanks. I should have them more often when I get spoiled like this."

The three of them were halfway through lunch before Skye remembered she hadn't told them that Julian had been found. It had been a challenge to think clearly all morning with the little sleep she'd gotten last night.

"Shoot. I haven't told you. Julian called Camille last night. We went and picked him up in Greenville." Skye wiped her fingers in a napkin, debating whether to have another sandwich or a piece of pie. "He was in the hospital after a car accident."

"Good lord. Why didn't the hospital contact his brothers?" her momma asked.

"They were just keeping him for observation for a concussion, and in case there was any internal bleeding. It was completely up to Julian to call or not."

"Those poor boys." Her momma sighed. "They're so lost."

"Angry," Skye corrected as she helped herself to the pie. "And they don't know the anger comes from bottled up grief. Instead of leaning on each other, they take it out on whichever brother's closest."

The bell signaling someone had come through the front door of the clinic rang, and her daddy rose. "I've got it. Stay and finish your lunch, honey."

Skye smiled at him. "Thanks, Daddy."

"I got you something," her momma said and handed her a present wrapped in gold paper.

"But you and Daddy already got me the purse and the watch."

"I know, but I saw this last week and just had to get it for you. Open it."

Feeling thoroughly spoiled after getting the cutest purse and a gold watch, as well as a gorgeous, colorful scarf from her brother, she opened the present. Inside she found a beautifully decorated leather binder. It looked antique.

"For your songs," her momma said.

"Oh, Momma." Tears welled up in her eyes. Why had she been so adamant about keeping her songwriting success to herself? Her momma thought it was just a little hobby, and still she'd gotten Skye the most stunning binder for it.

She had the perfect way of making her parents proud of her, and then she just kept it to herself. Skye suddenly felt very ashamed of her selfishness.

"Do you like it?"

"I love it. Thank you." Skye rose and went over to hug her momma. She'd change some things in her life, including the way she kept such a big part of herself from the people she loved.

"Look who I found," her daddy announced as he came back. "And he's not even sick."

Skye looked up to see Cameron appear in the door. "Hey."

"Hi."

Her momma rose and started gathering the dishes she'd brought. "It's good to see you, Cameron. Bertram dear, you'll help me get this out to the car, won't you? I'll see you later, Skye. Enjoy your day."

"Thanks, Momma. For lunch and for everything." She watched with amusement as her parents bustled out.

"Subtle," Cameron commented. "I didn't mean to chase them out. I just came to say thanks again for bringing Straw home."

"You're welcome. I didn't do much except keep Camille company."

He nodded. "I've thanked her, too."

"How's Julian this morning?"

"As annoying as ever. That knock he got to his head didn't do any good unfortunately." Cameron sighed and leaned against the doorframe. "We tried talking to him this morning, but...I don't know. I doubt it did any good."

"All you can do is try. Keep trying."

"We will." He held out a small present. "Happy birthday. I didn't think of it last night although it was technically past midnight by the time you came by."

Skye looked at the present, wrapped in dark blue paper and a silver bow. "Cam, you don't have to."

Without warning, he flashed her a killer smile. "Just open it whenever, okay? I gotta get back to work. We got a late start today. See ya."

And then he was gone. Skye never knew exactly what to expect from him. Like the present in her hand. What did that mean? They weren't friends...exactly. And she'd already told him that they couldn't be more than friends. So why was he getting her a birthday present? Infuriating man. Her curiousness won the battle against her stubbornness, and she ripped off the paper. Inside a little velvet pouch there was a thin silver necklace with a heart pendant. Music notes were etched on the heart, and she quickly recognized them as some from a song she'd written a lifetime ago down by the river. She'd written it, Cameron had played it on his guitar, and she'd thought she was the happiest girl in the world.

And dammit, now he'd made her cry.

\* \* \* \*

"You could at least have cooked dinner," Reid said to Straw as he and Cameron walked into the kitchen and found Straw drinking beer at the kitchen table.

"I'm injured," Straw defended himself.

"And you'll be plenty more injured if you don't start pulling your weight around here," Cameron told him. "If you're well enough to drink, you're well enough to cook a damn meal. Besides, I don't think you should be mixing those pain pills of yours with alcohol."

"Stay out of my business." Straw grabbed his beer and limped out. Then came back in. "Would it fucking kill you to ask how I'm doing? All you do is bitch about me not cooking, not cleaning, not calling. Did it ever occur to you that maybe I didn't want to talk to you? You actually think I wanted to be in hospital, and have you show up to blame me, or taunt me, or whatever you'd have done? Those few days in hospital were the most peaceful I've had in fucking years."

"Well, that told us, didn't it?" Reid snorted. "Poor Straw."

"Fuck you." Straw flipped them off and disappeared.

Cameron and Reid looked at each other, not needing to verbalize the issue. Who was going to make dinner?

"I made breakfast," Cameron pointed out.

"Shit."

Satisfied, Cameron went upstairs to shower and change. He could hear the usual obnoxious music from Straw's room and wondered if there was a way to actually get through to him or if he was a lost cause.

The latter didn't appeal to Cameron. He'd never been really close to Straw, the six-year age difference too much to form a bond when they'd been kids. When they'd gotten the chance with Straw coming of age, Cameron had been too busy with his own agenda to even notice that his youngest brother wasn't a snot-nosed brat anymore. It was with regret that he looked back and realized that none of them had ever given Straw the time of day. And now when they were trying to, Straw wasn't having it. Who could blame him?

While getting dressed after his shower, Cameron's thoughts strayed to Skye. He wondered if she'd opened the present he'd dropped off for her. He wasn't about to admit to her that he'd had it for years. He'd seen in in a store window in Nashville and impulsively bought and had it engraved, even though he'd hardly been able to afford it at the time. Originally it had been the plan to mail it to her for her birthday three or four years ago, but in the end he hadn't. Too much time had passed. Maybe too much time had still passed, but the need for her had never burned stronger inside of him than it did now.

Cameron blew out a breath. Life wasn't about what you wanted, it was about what you pried out of it despite the odds. He wasn't convinced he had it in him to pry something as magnificent as Skye Jones out of life's grasp and keep her for himself. Sometimes he didn't even know if he should try. But he wanted to. Oh, but he wanted.

Hunter came out of his room just as Cameron was heading down to investigate if dinner was ready. He was starving.

"You think now's a good time to have that talk about the tasks at the mill?" Hunter asked.

"I don't know. Straw's got his panties in a twist because we haven't asked about his aches and pains."

Hunter frowned. "I guess we haven't, but only because Skye told us he was relatively okay."

"Which Straw doesn't know," Cameron concluded.

"Great. On top his usual moodiness, we now also have to deal with his feelings being hurt. Anyone would think we had a sister."

"Maybe we really should start calling him Jules again. Or maybe Julia."

Snickering, they went downstairs just in time for one of Reid's weird fish dishes being put on the table. Cameron figured Reid had been sailing too long. His fish stews or whatever he called them were full of coconut, chili, and ingredients normal people had never even heard of. Where Reid got them was a mystery because there were no specialty shops in Maeville selling the stuff they ate whenever Reid was cooking. Maybe his boat was full of weird things he'd picked up from all over.

Straw didn't appear until the others were halfway through the meal. Face twisted in a permanent sneer, he sat down and frowned at his plate. "When are you going to cook something other than fish?"

"Says the fisherman," Reid said dryly. "Shut up and eat. Or do something useful, like perhaps cooking when it's your turn. This isn't a hotel."

"Good, then I won't tip you."

"Did you hurt your mouth in that accident of yours?" Hunter asked.

"No." Straw frowned. "Why? You suddenly interested in how I'm doing?"

"No, not particularly. I can hear you're just fine, and since your mouth isn't hurt, I suppose there's nothing stopping you from eating the dinner Reid went through the trouble of cooking. You'll need your strength for the dishes later and work tomorrow. I think you've officially used up all your sick days."

Cameron bit his lip trying not to laugh. Hunter had been so matter of fact that he'd apparently managed to do what no one had been able to before. He'd shut Straw up. The talk about the mill could wait.

\* \* \* \*

As a birthday present, Skye gave herself a quiet night in. She'd indulged in an early dinner with Camille and then taken refuge in her own home with her pajamas and a glass of wine. It wasn't the most spectacular of birthdays, but it was exactly what she needed. And if a birthday girl couldn't indulge herself, who could?

She was dozing on the couch, relaxing to some soothing music, when her phone rang. Too lazy to check who it was, she let it ring. Then it rang again, and she picked it up to see André's name on the display. That made her take the call because she knew he'd call until she answered.

"Hey, birthday girl. Out partying?"

She laughed. "No. Which makes me happy you're far, far away, because you'd probably have dragged me out somewhere whether I wanted it or not."

"You know it. Happy birthday, Skye. How was your day?"

"Thanks. It's been a quiet day, which is exactly what I wanted."

"You're getting old. A quiet day? Seriously, that's almost a crime when you're young and beautiful," he complained.

"Last night was eventful enough to last me a while. A friend's emergency created a little drama. Ended well, though. I think."

"Life in smalltime America," he said dryly.

"Shut up."

"All right, but then how can I tell you that we're nominated for another award? I really wish you'd consider coming down for the show and come with me on stage to accept it."

A thrill shot through Skye. They'd received awards before, but it never failed to excite her even though she had no intentions of accepting any, or boast about them. She didn't even have the actual statuettes, but that was okay because André liked "babysitting" them. All over the house to his wife's dismay. Skye knew she needed to share her success with the people she knew, but as far as the rest of the world was concerned, she wanted to be nothing more than a nurse in their eyes. The fame Cameron had been after, the fame that André thrived in, was not something she could ever cope with. It wasn't in her personality.

"You said nominated. We haven't won yet. Besides, we have a deal, and it's your pretty face on the front page of that deal."

"Awww. You think I'm pretty."

"And extremely silly. I don't know how Tracy puts up with you."

"Same way you do. I'm just that amazing."

Skye smiled to herself. His ego and silliness aside, André was a good friend—one she knew she could trust, and one who'd given her the break she needed to go after her big dream. "Goodnight, André. Time to go rest that ego."

He chuckled. "My ego doesn't need rest. Goodnight, Skye."

Ending the call, she felt more awake than she had all night. There went all her good intentions of going to bed early. Debating a little first, she spent ten minutes creating a short text to Cameron, thanking him for the present. She deleted and rewrote until she was satisfied that *thanks for the beautiful present, Cameron* conveyed what she wanted to say but none of the love she felt for him.

She groaned. She was worse than a teenager with a crush. Thanking someone for a thoughtful and beautiful present shouldn't take so long or involve that much doubt. She pressed *send* before she could question herself any further. When it was delivered, she wondered if she'd said enough.

"Ugh. Stop it," she said out loud to herself and got up from the couch. She'd go to sleep. Surely, when she was under the covers in the dark, her confused brain would remember it was tired and let her sleep.

She was part right, only it took her mind until after midnight to remember exactly how tired it was.

The following morning, the first patient at the clinic was Julian Madigan. Skye's protective instincts kicked into gear when she saw him and hurried over. "Julian. Are you okay?"

"No. I mean, yeah. I just need to see the doc."

"Are you in pain?"

"Look, I didn't come here to get quizzed. I just need to see the doc. That's what people who come here for, isn't it?"

"Yes, it is." Skye dug out her professional smile. "It's my job to ask, though. I'm a nurse, remember?"

He stared at her as if it hadn't occurred to him that she actually had a job at the clinic and didn't just hang around all day to pester people with questions she had no business asking. She'd gotten that reaction before, although it was a while ago. Everyone in Maeville had finally realized she was a fully trained nurse and not just Doc's little Skye. Well, almost everyone.

"Can I see the doc?" Julian asked, more calmly than before. "I've run out of pain pills, but my ribs are still killing me."

"I'll let him know you're here."

Skye went into her daddy's office conflicted. "Daddy? Julian Madigan is here to see you. Whatever pain medication they prescribed for him at the hospital in Greenville has run out, and he says he's still in pain."

"Okay, send him in, honey." He tilted his head when Skye didn't move away from the door. "Unless…is there something else?"

Skye bit her lip. "I don't know. Rumor has it he's doing drugs as well as getting drunk. I just…well, I'd really hate if we fed an addiction. And I know it's unprofessional to listen to rumors, but I'm worried about him."

Her daddy nodded thoughtfully. "I hear what you're saying. I'll have a talk with him, examine his ribs, and then go from there. If I think it's necessary, I'll prescribe a small dose of painkillers, and then maybe take a few minutes to call the hospital in Greenville. But for now, just show him in."

"Okay." Slightly less worried, she went back to the waiting room to get Julian. Her daddy would know what to do.

A little while later, Julian left looking pretty satisfied, even offered a small wave as he left the clinic. The worry returned, but Skye was determined to trust her daddy. He'd never let a patient down in the thirty years he'd run the clinic, and he had a way of getting to the bottom of every case and finding out what the patient needed rather than what they thought they needed.

# Chapter Sixteen

"Screw you."

Cameron sighed and bit back the reply threatening to escape. It wasn't very nice, and he was supposed to be diplomatic. Nice. Hunter's orders. Cameron wondered why Hunter was suddenly the boss of everyone. "It's not an ambush. It's mill business, and we need you there."

"Screw. You."

"Yeah, screw you, too." Yanking Straw's arm around his back, he had his younger brother screaming in pain and standing on his toes to escape the torture. "Stop squealing."

"Dammit, Cam! That shit hurts."

"So do my ears listening to you. Move." Not bothering to be gentle about it—he *had* asked Straw politely four times, after all—Cameron steered Straw toward the office where Hunter and Reid waited. Possibly Camille, too, if Hunter had managed to talk her into being part of the meeting.

"I'm not fucking going," Straw objected while occasionally hissing in pain.

"Seems like you are to me. Look down at your feet and tell me I'm wrong."

"I hate you."

Cameron laughed. "Lord, you really are ten years old, aren't you?"

When they got to the office, Cameron let go of Straw and pushed him into the room. Then stepped inside himself and locked the door behind him. The key went into his pocket.

"You nearly broke my arm, you ape." Straw was rubbing his elbow.

Hunter shook his head. "Cam, I told you to ask nicely."

"I did. Four times. I just didn't like his answer." Cameron sat down in one of the six chairs around the small conference table.

"I admire your problem solving skills," Camille told him. She was already seated at the head of the table looking slightly amused.

Cameron smirked. "Thanks, sugar."

"What's she doing here?" Straw wanted to know.

"Same as you are," Cameron replied. "She was just a big girl and could walk here herself."

Reid, never one to conform on the norm, sat on one end of the table, and Hunter stood in the middle, heading the meeting as the big boss he thought he was. Cameron couldn't decide whether that was an annoyance or a relief. Though, maybe it was just natural since he'd been the only one to ever really take an interest in the mill.

"It's time we sort some things out. Divide the responsibility and the various tasks. So far, we've been going about things as if it was just a temporary thing. I don't know what will happen when the year Daddy stipulated in his will is up, but I know we can't focus on it now. The mill has been doing well the last decade, and if we want that to continue, we have to be serious about what we do and act as if the four of us working here together is a permanent thing."

"Is this where we applaud?" Straw asked.

"What is it you want?" Hunter asked, tiredly letting himself fall into a chair. "No matter what anyone says or does, you're being a brat about it. And if that's what you want, then fine. Go be a brat. Then the adults will do the work for you, pick up the slack for you, and look the other way while you drink yourself to death or get locked up. Go."

Straw stayed in his seat.

"All right then." Hunter looked around. "Anyone else got any complaints before we continue?"

No one said anything, which was lucky, because if they had, Cameron was afraid he'd have punched them. Well, except maybe if it had been Camille.

"I think we should try to divide the responsibility so there are no crossed wires. Then maybe have weekly meetings or have Camille — if that's okay, of course — keep track of things. I think it's important that none of us — and by none of us, I really mean me — come across as the boss."

"Gee," Straw muttered but shut up when Cameron glared at him.

"So, does anyone want to share which part of the operation they prefer? It would be great if we could agree on this." Hunter looked around.

It was a long and painful meeting. Camille made coffee twice, and there were several bathroom breaks. The longer they talked and discussed— and, okay, argued—the less Straw sneered. Sometimes Cameron even forgot to listen to what was being said because he was seeing a whole new side to Straw, a side that discussed rationally without the ugly sneers and bratty remarks.

"So, do we agree? Hunter asked finally. "In addition to helping out where it's needed, Reid is our sales guy, Cam is in charge of the yard and the workers, Straw will manage the transportation and logistics, and I'll stay with the furniture like I have all along. Camille runs the office and keeps us in check."

"And I get this office," Reid added gleefully and rubbed his hands.

"It doesn't float, you know," Cameron reminded him. "You can't sail it."

"Yet." Reid snickered.

"Guys?" Hunter prodded.

"Yes, we agree," Reid said.

Cameron nodded.

"I don't have a say, but thanks for giving me one anyway," Camille said, gathering the notes she'd been taking. "I'm onboard."

"Well?" Hunter asked the suddenly quiet Straw.

"Sure. I just..." He rubbed his forehead.

Cameron guessed the problem and suddenly felt extremely protective of his youngest brother. "It's okay to ask questions. I'm betting Camille knows everything there is to know about this place."

Straw said nothing, but the fact that he didn't deny that had been his issue told Cameron he'd been right in his guessing.

Reid rose. "And now onto more important things. Lunch."

Cameron stayed behind in the office. He hoped it wasn't a mistake to give Straw more responsibility, though they'd all be there to make sure he didn't mess it up. And it was one of the few things they hadn't tried yet.

He stretched and toyed with the idea of driving into town and stopping by the clinic to ask Skye out for lunch. He had a hankering to look at her. Grinning, he jumped up. Yep. Time to go see the beautiful Skye.

\* \* \* \*

Cameron was the last person Skye wanted to see in the waiting room when she went to check if there were any more patients to see before her lunch break. She was frazzled, and everything—as in absolutely every little thing—had been going wrong from the moment she'd woken up that morning. She needed a break, and she needed to take care of the most important thing she'd ever had to take care of. Cameron being there ruined everything.

"You sick?" she asked, forgoing saying hello. "Hurt?"

"No, I'm fine. I ju—"

"Anyone else sick or hurt?" Skye interrupted.

"No, everyone's fine as far as I know. I wanted to a—"

"Sorry, I'm really busy. Can you do it later?"

Cameron laughed. "Can I ask you to lunch later? Sure, but since it's lunch time now, I'd really prefer to do it now."

That stopped her dead for a moment. Of all the times for Cameron to ask her out, now was the worst. And she couldn't even tell him why. In fact, she'd rather die, walk over hot coals, and go through some sort of water torture than tell him why. "Sorry, Cam. I…it's a really bad time."

"Are you okay?" The worry on his face did a number on her heart.

"Yeah." She took a deep breath and tried to calm down. "I just have something urgent to take care of."

"All right. I'll talk to you later then."

She nodded and managed a smile. When he'd left, she blew out a breath and turned her face upward. "Why me?" Then she snorted. She knew why. It was because she was weak and without a functioning defense against the man she loved. The man she compared every other man to. The man who needed to pull a John Travolta and shape up. The man she wanted and needed but was afraid to have.

Grabbing what she needed, she locked herself in the bathroom. Thankfully, her daddy had gone home for lunch, so he wouldn't question her weird behavior. Then she took the test that might change her entire life.

Skye had been close to calling in sick that morning upon waking up and barely making it to the bathroom before emptying her stomach. While dry-heaving into the toilet and reaching for the Kleenex under the sink, she'd made eye contact with the unopened box of tampons. She was late. So she'd vomited again.

A little later her stomach had felt fine, but she'd been so thoroughly distracted and freaked out that everything else had gone wrong. She'd burned her hand on the hot water for her tea, spent fifteen minutes looking for the keys she certainly didn't remember putting in the fridge, and stepped in not one, not two, but three puddles on the way to work, meaning she had to change into a new pair of scrubs upon arrival. Twenty minutes late. It was a small wonder her daddy hadn't taken one look at her and sent her back home.

As she waited for her fate to be determined, she thought back to the night she'd spent with Cameron. She'd never questioned if they'd been careful. Cameron had always been careful. She'd always been careful.

When they were younger, she suspected their carefulness stemmed from the same place—Cameron not wanting to get tied down, and her not wanting to hold him back. The words had never been spoken, but everything had been about his dreams back then. Well, their dreams until he'd taken them for his own.

Skye still didn't want to tie Cameron down. And she very much doubted he wanted to be tied down either. She swallowed thickly as she thought about it. Cameron's baby. She'd want it. If it was there, she'd want it more than anything. Something made out of love could not be killed. Her breath was unsteady as she struggled to get a hold on her nerves. She had no idea what she'd do or how she'd manage. But she would. And it wouldn't include doing something stupid like letting Cameron win her over when she was emotional and irrational. She'd have to be strong if she had to.

If…

Skye looked at her watch, then down at the sink where her future lay trapped in a little stick.

Negative.

Not pregnant.

The breath whooshed out of her body, and she sat down on the closed toilet lid. Then she started crying, part from relief, part from…no, she wasn't going to admit that part. Not even to herself.

When she'd sobbed out her emotions, she took a deep breath and decided she was done crying in the bathroom. Done thinking about babies that didn't exist. Done with… She sniffled. She wasn't done with anything. Her life, which she'd so carefully formed the way she wanted it to be, had gone cattywampus since Cameron's return. And there wasn't a thing she could do about it.

She took the time to wash her face and apply some light makeup to mask that she'd been crying before leaving the bathroom.

She skipped lunch, feeling a bit queasy. Then sat down at the desk and started overhauling the clinic's website, knowing the html would keep her thoughts from straying. If they did, she'd just start crying again.

* * * *

"Cam, for fuck's sake!"

Sliding the earmuffs down, Cameron turned to see a red-faced Reid striding across the yard. "What?"

"I've been yelling at you for five minutes to turn that noise down. I've got an important meeting, and I can't hear myself think, let alone what the potential *big* customer is saying."

"How about closing the door? This is a sawmill, not the financial district." Cameron put the earmuffs back on and continued sawing. He was pretty sure that if he hadn't been standing at the big circular, Reid would have swung at him. Sucked to be the little brother.

While he worked, Cameron thought about Skye. She'd been decidedly off kilter at lunch. Maybe he should pick up a pizza and drop by her place after work. Like old times. Except nothing was like old times, including him not being welcome at her place like he once had. He'd made damn sure of it with his leaving. And now he regretted it. Regretted sacrificing one dream for another when he technically didn't have to. Because Skye had been his dream, possibly even longer than music and fame had. And she was still his dream. A bright, shining star who'd made him happier just by being around since he'd come back to Maeville. It was time to show her, he decided. Time to show her how much she meant to him. Maybe their ship had sailed a long time ago, maybe it hadn't. And maybe, just maybe, it was returning to port after a six-year trip.

It was late that night before Cameron could escape the mill. One of the workers had twisted his ankle, and while Straw drove the guy in to see the doctor, Cameron had to fill in and make sure the orders were filled and the trucks loaded properly. It meant that his plan about picking up a pizza and going to see Skye fell through. She'd have eaten already. So he headed home, showered, and stuck his head into the kitchen to see if there was any dinner.

"It's your turn to cook," Hunter told him, pushing him out of the way as he came in loaded with grocery bags. "And I know we're four men living together, but this place could use some Christmas decorations."

"Actually, I was just headed out."

"Head out later. We need food."

Because he was hungry himself, he sighed and started unpacking the grocery bags. He hoped Hunter had bought something that was easy to fix so he could get out of there. No such luck, though. So Cameron made pork chops and gravy along with enough mashed potatoes to feed a small army. Which, he thought to himself, the Madigans probably looked like at times.

While he cooked, he could hear arguments, curses, and laughter coming from the living room. Unaccustomed to the combination, he went to investigate and found his brothers digging through boxes full of Christmas decorations.

"It looks like butt cheeks." Reid snickered and held up Cameron's third grade reindeer Christmas ornament.

"When was the last time you saw butt cheeks with horns?" Hunter asked.

"Well, you know that girl you dated in junior high?" Reid chortled and jumped out of the way as Hunter threw a headless Santa at him.

"They're antlers," Cameron said flatly. "Reindeer have antlers, not horns. Don't you know anything?"

They all turned to look at him. Then looked at the ornament. "It's a reindeer?" Straw asked.

Cameron sighed and went back to the kitchen. The laughter filling the living room behind him made him smile, though.

The mood was good during dinner. Even Straw was cracking jokes and unable to keep a straight face as he insulted Cameron's cooking. Reid was wearing a Santa hat, and they were busy rehashing Christmas memories, especially the embarrassing ones, which there were a lot of, when the doorbell chimed.

"I'll get it," Reid said, getting up.

"Remember when we got up late on Christmas Eve and switched all the tags on the presents around?" Hunter asked.

Cameron grinned. Things had been so simple back then— long before dreams had started tugging at himself and Reid, before Straw was anything more than a moody child, and before Hunter thought he was the boss of everyone. "Straw bawled when he thought Daddy had gotten the remote control car he'd wanted all year."

"I didn't bawl," Straw objected. "I'd gotten something in my eye."

"Yeah, tears," Hunter agreed.

Cameron's laughter died in his throat when he looked up and saw Skye and Reid coming into the kitchen. "Hi."

"Hi, guys. Sorry for interrupting your dinner."

"That's okay," Hunter assured her. "Have a seat. If you haven't eaten yet, there's plenty. Cam's not as bad a cook as one might expect of a country star."

Cameron made sure to avoid Skye's gaze. It was awkward to hear his own lie, or rather omission of the truth repeated by Hunter, when Skye knew the truth.

"Thanks, but I already ate. I just came by to talk to Cameron. I can wait while you finish your dinner."

He rose from the table and put his plate in the sink. "I'm done. Do you want something to drink at least?"

"Yeah, thanks. If you've got something sweet."

She'd always preferred sweet beverages. In the past, he'd have told her that she didn't need anymore sugar because she was already plenty sweet. He'd probably have said it again now if his brothers hadn't been watching them as if they'd bought tickets for the show. So he just grabbed two sodas and led Skye to the music room. No one had used it but Cameron when they were all kids, and he'd avoided it like the plague since coming back because of all the memories it held. But now it seemed appropriate. Plus, it was one of the rooms furthest away from the kitchen and the living room.

"You okay?" he asked Skye as they sat down in the couch in there. The place needed a proper dusting, but he couldn't remember whose turn it was to clean this week. Just that it wasn't his.

"Yeah. Well, I guess." She toyed with the soda without opening it. "I've been debating all afternoon whether to tell you this or not. I mean, there's no reason to, except that if the result had been different, I would definitely have told you. So why shouldn't I tell you just because it turned out to be false alarm? Ultimately, I'm just being selfish because I don't want to be the only one who knows...even though there's not actually anything to know. And I don't want to tell anyone but you. Besides, we've told enough lies and skirted enough truths."

"Okay..." Cameron had rarely heard Skye ramble, and he was more than just a little intrigued. And, he discovered a second later, completely unprepared for what she had to say.

# Chapter Seventeen

"Earlier today when you stopped by, I was freaking out because I thought I might be pregnant."

"You … what? Seriously?"

Cameron stared at her until it was like he was staring through her, completely lost in his own thoughts. Skye could hardly blame him, considering her own freak-out. So she gave him a few minutes although she was itching to know what was going through your head.

"Well, hell," he finally said and reached for her hand. "I don't know what kind of reaction you're expecting, but I'm kind of…I don't know."

"Yeah, I know what you mean." The palm-to-palm contact, innocent as it was, did a number on her heart at the same time as it calmed her down as few other things could. His touch just felt right, and she swallowed the contented sigh threatening to escape.

"Remember when we used to make plans for the future? First we'd do this, then we'd do that. We had it all mapped out. Struggling artists, success, marriage, kids." She nodded, afraid the lump in her throat would make it impossible for her to talk. "I've never said it, which I should have, but I'm sorry for ruining it. More sorry than I'll ever be able to express. The dream of success blinded me, I guess, and somewhere deep down I was afraid you wouldn't want to come after all. You seemed so happy with your studies."

"I'd have come with you," she managed. Whatever she'd expected from telling him about her scare earlier, it wasn't the heart to heart a part of her had yearned for.

"Would you have been happy?" He barked out a laugh that held no mirth. "And that's a stupid thing to ask one half of the most successful songwriting duo in the country music business. I guess what I meant was if you'd have been happy with me."

"I can't answer that, Cam." Skye sighed. "If you'd asked me to come, you might have started to resent me if I'd found success and you hadn't. Or maybe you'd have been successful because we'd have worked together. I'd have had your back unlike those people you ended up trusting with your talent and your career. On the other hand, I might also have crashed and burned, never finding the chance that André gave me if I'd gone about it differently. But ultimately, we'll just never know what could have been. Just what is."

"No," he agreed solemnly. "We won't. Just like we'll never know where we'd have ended up if you really had been pregnant. It's probably silly, but there's a part of me that's disappointed."

She squeezed his hand and admitted the truth. "Me too. And that's ridiculous since we can't be more than friends, Cam."

"So you keep saying."

"I'm lying, you're lying. It's a good thing I'm not pregnant because a baby deserves better than that. And so do we. Lies are a bad foundation for a relationship."

"I bet I could convince you differently." The hand that held her tugged her closer. A glint in those dark blue eyes warned her that he was up to something, but she was still surprised when he yanked her into his lap. He leaned in to place a feather light kiss beneath her ear.

"Beautiful Skye." His breath tickled her sensitive skin, and her eyes closed involuntarily. If he'd told her to go jump from a tall bridge, she'd have done it. His hand felt scorching against her thigh, and her breath hitched when she felt his lips against her own for the shortest of moments.

"Cam, please."

"Please what?" His other hand traveled up her body until his thumb rubbed against the underside of her breast. He was driving her crazy.

"Just please."

When their lips met again, she pressed closer, letting her fingers thread into his hair beneath the messy knot at the back of his head. She couldn't get enough of him—his taste, his touch, his scent. Everything that was bad for her was exactly what she wanted. Needed. Craved.

"Oh, shit. Sorry. Never mind me."

Skye opened her eyes as Cameron pulled away. She saw Reid's sheepish smile before the door closed again. She hadn't even heard it open. Her hands fell down to her sides as her gaze met Cameron's briefly. She climbed off his lap and retreated to the end of the couch while making a conscious effort not to lick her lips.

"I should go," she said before looking up, fully expecting not to meet his gaze. But she did—and the hunger in his eyes took her breath away.

"If you think you have to. I'd really like it if you stayed, though."

The naked honesty took her by surprise, and she'd nearly said okay before remembering her promises to herself. She'd come to be honest with him amidst the lies they continued to live in a web of, not to make a bigger mess of her life than she already had. She didn't even know if Cameron was staying or going when the year stipulated in his daddy's will was up. She didn't know what his plans were or what he really wanted now that he'd realized he couldn't have what he had dreamed of. If he expected her to be his consolation prize, he could think again.

"I really think I have to," she said as she rose from the couch. "Goodnight, Cam."

Skye was aware that she was practically fleeing, and though it was a hit to her pride, it was necessary for her sanity. There was every chance that she'd end up staying as long as Cameron wanted her to if she didn't get out right now. She was more than just a little grateful that she didn't run into any of his brothers, but she supposed Reid had already filled them in, anyway.

Putting on her boots and grabbing her coat, she burst out of the door and took a deep breath of cold night air. Dear lord, she was in trouble. And she'd already dodged one bullet today.

* * * *

Cameron stayed in the music room. He could still taste Skye on his lips, but it was more than her taste that filled his thoughts. Frustration raged through him, his body all but vibrating for her.

Despite her abrupt exit when Reid interrupted them — and Cameron was planning on killing his younger brother for that later — her body had hinted that she wasn't as firmly against being with him again as her words suggested. He wondered if she knew what she wanted herself as she was steadily making him more and more confused. Perhaps it was his own fault for messing things up six years previously. It was no wonder if she was hesitant and scared that he'd do it again.

Then there was the reason for her weird behavior earlier at the clinic. A baby. Or the suspicion that there might have been one. He'd meant it when he'd said that there was a part of him that was disappointed. He'd never thought about marriage, kids, and growing old with anyone but Skye. And while it was no surprise that he still wanted that, the desperate need for it was more than just a little surprising. He was ready for all the things he'd thought he wouldn't want. A home, roots, a steady job, settling down with the woman he loved. A house full of kids, bikes in the driveway, toys on the floor. More than anything, he just wanted Skye to be his. Needed it. Craved it. And he'd fight for it.

Someone knocked on the door, and a moment later Reid stuck his head in. "Coast clear?"

"Now you ask. Bastard."

Reid snickered and came into the room. He sat down at the piano and pressed a couple of random keys. He didn't have a musical bone in his body. "So, what's up with you and Skye?"

"None of your business, brother."

"Come on."

Cameron shook his head. "Nope."

"Well, you suck. But since the lady's gone, why don't you come help us decorate?"

Cameron got up and collected the forgotten soda cans. "I'll take a rain check."

He swung by the kitchen while Reid went back to the living room, where Hunter and Straw appeared to be arguing about who'd made best looking paper elves as kids. Cameron knew the answer to that one. None of them.

The doorbell rang just as he passed through the hall. "I'll get it," he yelled, hoping it was Skye who'd changed her mind and not wanting an audience if she had.

It was not Skye outside the front door, however. At first he didn't even recognize the plump woman with the heavy makeup who offered him the most insincere smile he'd seen since the last time he'd talked to his old manager in Nashville.

"Oh my. It's Cameron, isn't it?" she asked.

It was the voice that did it for him. A nasal, grate-on-you-nerves voice he hadn't heard in years—and easily could have done without ever hearing again.

"Charlene," he greeted her flatly. He had never liked Straw's momma. Whatever the reason was for her standing on the Madigan front porch, it was not a good one. Most likely she wanted something, and whatever it was, it wasn't the one thing she ought to want. Her son.

"Oh, honey, I only just heard about your daddy the other day, and I came right up here. I'm so sorry."

"Thanks, Charlene. There was no need for you to make the trip, though." Last he'd heard, she was on marriage number three—or was it four?—and had just turned away Straw again. There was no way he was letting her into the house even though the manners he'd been taught demanded that he ask her in. He'd never learned to love his daddy's third wife, and considering what she'd done to Straw since the divorce, no Madigan owed her anything.

"I wanted to be there for Julian. Poor dear must be hurting."

"Poor dear was hurting long before his daddy died," Cameron replied and closed the door behind him, urging Charlene back. "And you'd know that since you caused some of that hurt."

"Why, I don't know what you could possibly mean by that." She flapped her hand in front of her face as though she was hot in the chilled night air. "I've merely come to console my son."

"Your son's just fine. And since we both know you're not here for him, I'll just tell you straight out that there's no inheritance that you can manipulate away from him. Daddy's will came with terms, terms that don't concern you. But there's no pocket money for you, so I suggest you leave. I really don't want Julian to see you."

"Why, I've never…! Aren't you just the rudest man!"

"I think the word you're looking for is *honest*, though I don't mind rude too much. As long as I get my message across. And it's this, Charlene: Go away. Leave Maeville and don't mess up Julian more than you already have."

"You Madigans are all alike," she seethed. "You think you're so much better than everyone else, but let me tell you something, Cameron Madigan. You're not. You're trash, and you can keep your precious little Julian."

He watched as she marched down the path and got into a dark sedan parked at the curb. It was no wonder Straw thought fate had screwed him over with a momma like that. Cameron decided not to tell him she'd stopped by. She'd done so before, and it had never been to see her son. It had been to beg, borrow, or steal money from her ex-husband. And whenever Straw had contacted her, she'd blown him off, claiming she was busy with her new life, her new husband, her new family. Everything had to be new to Charlene or she got bored with it. An angry child who needed his mother wasn't enough to hold her interest. Cameron had never known his own mother, but he knew that he'd gotten a better deal than Straw. Sighing, he went inside. Maybe he would go decorate the house with his brothers. He'd had enough of females for one night.

* * * *

It was with trepidation that Skye let Camille talk her into coming out to the sawmill and helping with the Christmas market that weekend. Ideally, she'd have liked to avoid Cameron a little longer. Mainly because she wasn't sure she'd be strong enough to resist him again, but also because she didn't know what to say to him.

It had probably been a mistake to go see him and to tell him about the pregnancy scare. But she'd needed to tell someone, and as tempting as it had been to call Camille and open a bottle of wine, it was Cameron's business a lot more than it was Camille's. If only things hadn't gotten out of hand. Thank God for Reid's interruption even if it had been embarrassing.

Skye took a deep breath before making the turn down the lane to the mill. No going back now. She was only there to sell candied apples or whatever booth Camille put her in charge of. She'd done it before and always enjoyed it. Today would be no exception.

It turned out she'd worried for nothing. She had been selling hot cider for more than an hour before she even saw Cameron, and he only gave her a distracted wave as he hurried past her.

"It's not you," Camille leaned over to whisper to her. She was selling candied apples next to Skye. "Cameron's on red alert because Charlene is back in town."

Skye frowned. "Why does Julian's momma being in town worry Ca—oh, she wants money. Bitch. How is Julian taking it?"

"He doesn't know. That's why Cameron is on red alert. He's trying to keep Julian from finding out." Camille stepped closer and lowered her voice even more. "He's been doing so well lately. Since we went and got him in Greenville, actually. I haven't seen him drunk once, and he's out here a lot more after he got more responsibility. Even his driving's improved now that he's driving his daddy's truck. Cameron pulled me aside this morning and asked me to look out for Charlene and let him know if I saw her. Though, truth be told, I'm not sure I'd recognize the hag."

"Me either," Skye muttered. Her memories of the third Mrs. Madigan were vague at best, though she'd heard plenty about her over the years. From Cameron and later from Hunter. She wondered if Cameron knew what message he was sending trying to protect Julian like that. It spoke of brotherly love and commitment.

Though she didn't know what she was looking for, Skye looked an extra time at every woman old enough to be Julian's momma. But she knew most of the people at the market, if not by name, then at least by their faces. Most were locals, and those who weren't didn't raise any red flags for her. She was almost disappointed. Being on the lookout kept her nicely distracted.

Camille was right about Julian, though. He stopped by for a cup of cider and showed off a rare but very charming side of himself. The smile and the Santa hat, which was the official sawmill uniform on Christmas market days, made an enormous difference. He had a blinding smile, and it transformed his face completely when he used it. Julian was quite simply a beautiful man. If you looked past his reputation and focused purely on his smiling face, you'd think he was an angel. Chiseled cheekbones, perfect skin, twinkling eyes. Those Madigans were something else.

Things were winding down, and Skye was warming her hands around a cup of cider. Most of the people had left, but there were still a few stragglers milling about. For some, it seemed like choosing the right Christmas tree was one of life's most important decisions. Skye already had a small one picked out for her cabin. It was waiting on her back porch to be carried inside and decorated. But not yet. There would be no needleless tree in her home for Christmas.

Not thinking anything of it, she watched a car drive down the lane and park in the area reserved for it. If people kept arriving after the official closing time, they'd never get to go home. As soon as the driver of the car exited the vehicle, Skye knew it was no customer, though. She didn't know what it was that looked familiar about the woman, and maybe she'd thought nothing of it if Camille hadn't told her about Julian's momma. But she was certain the woman in the impractical shoes and too short jacket was Charlene.

Candied apples having sold out, Camille had left to go and clear up some of the other booths. Skye didn't see her anywhere, nor any of the Madigans. Knowing Julian had been netting Christmas trees, Skye kept an eye on Charlene to make sure she didn't go around back. Then she sprinted across the yard and burst into the office. To her great relief, both Cameron and Hunter were there.

"Charlene's here," she managed to get out while trying to catch her breath.

Cameron said nothing as he hurried outside. Hunter patted her on the shoulder and shrugged. "Might as well go see the show. I don't know what he thinks he can do about Charlene if she's gotten the scent of money, but we might as well provide a little backup. Where's Straw?"

"Netting trees last I saw him, but that was a while ago."

"Kid's got enough problems without his momma hanging around. Damn, that woman has lousy timing."

Skye could only agree. Especially when she heard Julian yelling.

# Chapter Eighteen

"I'm fucking sick and tired of people trying to run my life and always telling me what to do, what not to do, and when to fucking do it. I'm sick of it."

Cameron let Straw rage. He wasn't going to apologize for wanting to protect his brother from the hot mess that was his momma, and he didn't care how anyone thought he'd handled it. He'd do it all over again if he had to. But right now all he wanted was to get Charlene the hell out of there.

"And you." Straw turned to gesture to his momma, who was looking a lot less comfortable with the situation than she had when Cameron had initially intercepted her heading for Straw. "You think you can just show up here after all the crap you've given me over the years every single fucking time I've reached out to you? And why now? Because Daddy died and you think you can cash in on that? You're delusional."

He shot out of there, heading for the woods. When Charlene took a step as if to follow him, Cameron stopped her. "No way. He doesn't want anything to do with you, and who can blame him? You've got five minutes to get off the property."

"But my baby boy…"

"If he was ever your baby boy, that was a hell of a long time ago. Now move it, lady."

Sniffing, she turned. Cameron thought she really was going to leave when she spotted Skye and Hunter.

"Hunter!" she wailed and produced a handkerchief. "Please help me. I just want to talk to Julian. Apologize. Make it up to him if I've hurt him."

"Charlene, why don't you stop the theatrics? We all know why you're here, but more than that, Julian is a grown man. If he says he doesn't want to talk to you—and I believe he just did quite clearly—then he's got every right. I also believe that when the owners of a property ask you to leave, then you leave. And Cameron just asked you to leave."

Leave it to Hunter to be polite even to trash, but at least he'd gotten her to leave. Of course, there was still Straw to deal with, and Cameron was afraid that they were back to square one with him. And things had been going so well lately, too. Damn Charlene.

"I'll follow her and make sure she actually leaves," Hunter said and headed for one of the ATVs.

Cameron nodded. Then winced as he realized that left him to go after Straw. "I'll just…" He gestured in the direction Straw had taken off in and wished things would just work out right once in a while. He finally had Skye alone for the first time today, and he had to go babysit his little brother. He'd been down that alley so many times it was laughable.

"Want me to come with you?" she asked.

A grin formed on his lips before he realized that was what he had been supposed to ask her six years ago. It might have been that easy. Or it might not have been. She was right— they'd never know. "Thanks. I'd like that," he said instead.

The light dusting of snow they'd gotten overnight made it easy to track Straw. Skye walked quietly beside him, looking cuter than should be allowed with her white knitted hat firmly tucked onto her head.

Maybe sometime soon they'd be able to take a walk that didn't include one of them running away from their problems or looking for Straw. Just walking down by the river like they used to do. A guy could always dream. Cameron smiled to himself. He hadn't dreamed in a long time, and it was only because of Skye that he'd started again.

"I'm sorry I didn't get to you in time."

He turned his head to look at her again. "What?"

"So you could keep Charlene away from Julian. It was a very nice thing to try and do for him."

"It's not your fault. And I didn't do it to be nice."

"Then why did you do it?"

"Because she's like a disease to him. He's family and she's not." And it really was that simple, he thought to himself. Straw might be a pain in the ass most of the time, but he was family. "She showed up at the house last night not long after you'd left. I managed to get her to leave, but I had a feeling she'd be back."

"Money-sniffing whore," Skye muttered.

Cameron burst out laughing. "Spot on."

They found Straw kicking the living daylights out of a tree. Why he'd chosen that particular tree Cameron had no idea, but it was receiving his full wrath. He and Skye stayed back and let Straw get it all out. After a few minutes, he limped over to the next tree and slid down until he was sitting with his back against it and his knees drawn up to his chest.

"Is she gone?" he asked.

"Yep. Hunter followed her to make sure," Cameron replied, waiting for the anger and the sneers to be directed at him, as well.

Straw stared right ahead. "She's been here before?"

"At the house last night." Cameron might have wanted to shield Straw from her, but since that had gone belly up, he went with the truth.

"And she wanted money?"

"No offense, but isn't that the only thing she wants?" Cameron sighed. "Like today, she tried to make it sound like she wanted to be there for you, blah, blah, but we all know what she's like."

"Yeah." Straw blew out a breath. "We all know."

"It's cold out here," Skye said gently. "You think you can walk back on that foot or do you need me to get an ATV?"

"Foot's fine," Straw muttered and got up. Although he tried not to show it, every step made him wince, and he limped slightly.

"Stay there. I'll get an ATV," Skye said.

"He's fine," Cameron stated, going over to Straw and offering him a shoulder to lean on. After a moment, Straw put his arm around Cameron's shoulder and they started walking. "He just said so."

"Lord save me from stubborn males," Skye muttered behind them.

Cameron looked at Straw, and they shared a grin.

* * * *

After the eventful day at the sawmill, Skye was happy to have a quiet afternoon at home. She made hot chocolate to warm up from the inside out and dug through her cookie recipes. It was never really too early to start making Christmas cookies. If they were eaten before Christmas, it just gave you a reason to make more. And she loved baking.

She'd only just gotten started on kneading the dough when there was a rap on the kitchen window. At least it wasn't the doorbell, she thought to herself, as she looked from her dough-covered hands to the window. Cameron grinned at her through the glass.

Gesturing first to the bowl and then toward the door, she figured he got the message when he disappeared. A moment later she heard him come in the front door.

"Are you making cookies?" he asked even before he'd come into the kitchen.

"How did you know?"

"Instinct." He came in, hair still wet from the shower and looking like he had the same plans for the afternoon as she did. Relaxing. The worn jeans, knitted socks, and soft knitted sweater looked as comfortable as her yoga pants and sweatshirt were. She didn't even wish she was wearing better clothes or that she'd had on makeup. She'd never felt like she had to impress Cameron or pretend she was always a put-together person who never had a bad hair day and always looked as if she was ready for a meal at a semi-formal restaurant.

184

"Plus," he added, "it's December and you've got your hands in a bowl in the kitchen."

"I think you know me too well." Though, because they did know each other that well, Skye continued making the dough while Cameron made himself at home, getting a mug out of the cupboard and pouring himself some hot chocolate. He sat down at the kitchen table and watched her.

"How's Straw's foot?" Skye asked as she started scooping the dough onto a baking tray with two spoons.

"It's fine. Straw's fine. It's like Charlene was never here, which I suppose should worry me a bit. But at the moment he's resting his foot and making Reid and Hunter fetch him stuff. It was when he suggested that we get him a bell that I decided to get out of there."

Skye laughed. "I'm glad he's okay, but you're probably right that you should worry a bit. She's messed him up before, and just because he's an adult doesn't mean that she's lost the ability to hurt him."

Cameron hummed in agreement. "Hey, what's that?" he asked and pointed to the window.

She looked but saw nothing out of the ordinary. When she turned her head back toward the baking tray and Cameron, he was grinning and chewing. A scoop of dough was missing from the plate.

"Seriously?" She shook her head but couldn't keep the smile off her face. It was an old routine. "You want to lick the spoon next?"

"Yes, please. Both of them."

"You get one."

"And the bowl," he negotiated.

"There will be no licking bowls in my kitchen." Then laughed when she heard the words coming out of her mouth. "You're a bad influence, Cameron Madigan. Mind telling me what you're doing here?"

He leaned back in the chair and watched her with a look in his eyes she wasn't sure what to make of. "Last night got me thinking. Perhaps it could be you and me."

Careful to keep her facial expression as neutral as possible, she put the tray in the oven and set the timer. "Perhaps it could."

Cameron leaned forward. "But you don't really think so?"

"No." Skye felt her heart breaking down the middle. "The thing is, Cam...I love who you are, but as long as you don't, there's no future for us. I've come to terms with my lie, and I know I need to let people in. You haven't, and essentially you've wasted a decade. Not on failed dreams — dreams fail every day — but on self pity or vanity."

He studied her silently for a few minutes. Then nodded. "Well, I guess you told me. You love me, but I'm not good enough."

"That's not what I said," Skye objected.

"Sure it is. You can lie, but I can't."

"I've never had any need to shout from the rooftops who I am and what I can do. Fame was your dream."

"Our dream," he corrected her.

"Okay, our dream. Maybe I'd have been okay with the fame if I could have shared it with you. But you took that choice away from me, so I did it my own way. People write under pen names all the time. It's normal. Pretending to be a star when you're not is not normal. It's not healthy."

"What the hell do you want me to do? I can't stop people from assuming things." He sprang up and started to pace in her small kitchen. "You want me to put an ad in the paper and announce to the good people of Maeville that Cameron Madigan is an epic failure? You want me take Rob up on his offer and start singing at the bar on Saturdays for free beer?"

"I think you'd be happier if you did. Not the ad, but the singing. You used to love it. It shouldn't matter if it's on a big stage in Nashville, or if it's at the local bar in Maeville."

"You love writing, so you'd be happy writing limericks for the local radio station?" he challenged her.

"I'd still write even if Nashville decided they didn't want me anymore. If it was for the local radio station or my desk drawer, I'd write because I love it."

"Well, I guess you're just a better person than I am then."

He walked out of the kitchen and out of the cabin. Skye desperately hoped he wasn't walking out of her life, because even though she didn't think their outlooks on life meshed very well, she felt tears prickling in her eyes at the thought of not having him in her life in some capacity. She already knew what it was like to be without him, and her heart had been dead for those six years.

Frustrated, she yanked out the cookies when the timer went off but didn't put the next tray in. Instead she went to the window and stared out without seeing anything. If only she didn't love him. It was cruel to love someone that you knew wasn't good for you. Living a lie had to stop, and if she stopped her own lying, it would do her no good to start living Cameron's lie.

\* \* \* \*

Angrily, Cameron marched along the river. What the hell did he expect? That someone as exceptionally beautiful, talented, and smart as Skye would go for a nobody like him?

A nobody with no education, no accomplishments, and hardly a dime to his name? The only reason he had a steady job and a home was because his daddy had died. Shit. Maybe he should start kicking trees like Straw. It seemed to have done his brother a world of good.

But she loved him, a voice told Cameron inside his head. Though, what was love but pain you couldn't cure with pills or alcohol?

He walked until it got dark. Then he walked some more. Not until he accidentally stepped into the water and had to deal with a waterlogged boot did he return home. The strings of Christmas lights either Reid or Hunter had strung around the porch railing were mockingly cheerful, and the inside of the house wasn't much better.

All the old decorations he remembered from when he was a kid sat around the whole house. Someone had even had the nerve to plant the ugliest Santa in the world—Cameron was pretty sure it was one Reid had made in the first or second grade—on the dresser in his room. It mocked him with its uneven smile and crooked hat.

Surveying his room, Cameron took stock of his meager belongings. Except for the guitar he'd inherited from the musically talented mother he'd never had a chance to get to know and the ring he'd bought years ago for Skye, he owned nothing of value. When he'd sold his valuables in Nashville, those were the two things he couldn't bear to part with, which was ironic since he'd vowed never to play the guitar again and the woman he'd bought the ring for didn't want him.

Which led him to question his sanity. He wanted Skye, yes. But did he deserve her...and did she deserve him? The latter was a big no. She deserved better. The real question was if he could be what she deserved...whatever that was. He rubbed his forehead. Lord, he wanted nothing more than a simple life that held some kind of meaning. Glancing at the guitar, he considered it for a moment. Did he still have it in him to play? He shook his head and left the room.

Straw was watching TV in the living room, and Hunter was in the kitchen cooking what looked like some sort of roast. When Cameron asked where Reid was, Hunter only offered a distracted "attic" as an answer. Too restless to sit down and wait for dinner, Cameron climbed the stairs to the attic and found Reid with cobwebs in his hair and half-buried in boxes.

"Redecorating?" Cameron asked.

Reid sneezed. "No, just looking for more Christmas lights. We used to have a big Santa and some reindeer."

"That was years ago."

"So? They could still be up here." Reid looked around. "A small village could be hidden up here and no one would know. Damn, there's a lot of stuff."

Cameron looked into the nearest box. It was full of pictures, and the one at the top was of his momma. He picked it up and gave it a sad smile. She'd been a beautiful woman and, he suspected, the true love of his daddy's life. He stuffed it in his pocket and looked in the next box. It too, held traces of the woman who had once been the mistress of the Madigan house.

His momma's jewelry box, which he remembered his daddy showing him when he was a boy, was perched on top of a bunch of clothes. Picking it up, he was surprised to find it still full. He'd have thought Charlene had cleaned the place out of every piece of jewelry. He put it aside for later. "Tell me where to look, Clark Griswold."

Reid grinned and sneezed again. "Could be fun, couldn't it? To light up the entire street. Or the whole town. You look over there, I'll continue here."

Fun, Cameron thought as opened another box. He doubted that very much, but he'd indulge Reid just to distract himself from thinking too much about his latest fiasco. If he was good at nothing else, he was good at those. Good at failing.

# Chapter Nineteen

Instead of brooding about Cameron, Skye spent a lot of time thinking about how to tell Camille and her parents, as well as Sebastian whenever she saw him next—they were the most important ones, although she supposed she'd want to tell Hunter, Sam, Wendy, and maybe a few other friends—that her little hobby was somewhat of a career. That she was, in fact, one of the most sought after songwriters in the country music business. She didn't think the "hey, guess what?" approach would be the best. So she compiled some of the biggest hits she and André had composed together on a CD and headed toward Camille's place.

Her best friend opened the door in her yoga outfit, took one look at Skye, and put her hands on her hips. "What's wrong?"

"Nothing."

"You look nervous."

"Seriously?" Camille had always had sharper instincts than anyone Skye had ever met, but she had to be a mind reader to know what Skye had planned. Or that she had anything planned at all.

"You're clutching that purse strap like it's a lifeline."

Skye looked down and relaxed her hand. Then smiled at Camille. "Your talents are wasted out at the mill. You should be a detective."

"No thanks. I'd find that too restrictive. Come on in, I was just about to reward myself with some coffee cake after my yoga routine."

"Actually, I was hoping to lure you over to my parents' place for a little while."

"And Mama Jones' Christmas cookies? Give me two minutes to change."

Fifteen—not two—minutes later they were heading up the road to Skye's parents' house.

"Is it bad news?" Camille asked. "Because if you're about to tell us you're dying or something awful like that, I'll kill you."

"I know you would, but it's not bad news."

"Thank the Lord. Good news?"

Skye shrugged. It was, but the fact that they were years too late might dampen the enthusiasm considerably. "It's news. News I should have told y'all ages ago."

"You're lucky I love you, and that I have enough patience not to either beat or tickle it out of you right now."

Skye grinned. "I really am."

She felt even luckier a little while later when the three of the most important people in her life—she ignored the little voice in the back of her mind that kept chanting Cameron's name—patiently listened when she asked them to.

"There is no excuse for keeping it to myself, but I guess my reason was fear that I'd fail and get my heart ripped open again. And then it just became…routine? I don't know what to call it. But it was something that was just mine. Something happened recently, though, that made me realize that I had to share it with you. I'll have to ask you not to tell anyone, though. I couldn't handle the consequences."

"Skye?" Camille asked. She was sitting with Skye's parents on the couch while Skye paced and talked.

"Yes?"

"Spit it out already."

"You're not in trouble, are you, honey?" her momma asked.

"No, I'm not. But I haven't been honest to you about my songwriting."

Her daddy rose from the couch. "It's not a shame to fail if you've given it your best."

Skye mentally reminded herself to ask her daddy to talk to Cameron sometime. Then she smiled. "I know, Daddy. But I'm not trying to tell you that I've failed. I'm trying to tell you the opposite."

The lack of reaction made her realize she needed to be more specific. "You've heard my songs on the radio. I make more money writing songs then I do nursing. A lot more."

"So you're famous?" Camille asked.

"My writing partner, André, and the pen name I write under are, yes. But I don't want the fame. I just want to write songs." She went over and started the music. Then watched as recognition dawned on their faces. Her parents especially kept looking from the stereo to her and back again. Camille seemed lost in her own thoughts.

After four songs, Skye turned the volume down and turned to face the verdict. There was pride welling up inside of her that she hadn't expected, but most of all she was nervous. She'd made her dream come true, but she'd waited years to share it with those closest to her. There was bound to be disappointment.

"I'm proud of you, honey, and happy for you. But I—no, we—would have been proud of you either way. You had the courage to go after your dream, and you did it responsibly." Her daddy came over and put an arm around her, then kissed her cheek.

"Thanks, Daddy."

"He's right," her momma agreed. "I suppose we thought it was just something you were fooling around with for fun. I'll want to listen to everything now."

"I'll get it for you," Skye promised. Two down, one to go, she said to herself as she studied Camille's expressionless face.

"I'm just thinking," Camille said when she noticed Skye's gaze. "I'm just thinking that I hope you've got a secret or two left because it suits you to be a little mysterious. Even to your parents and to your best friend. I'm also thinking that I'm proud of you. Not just for writing awesome songs, but for having the courage to tell us now when you didn't have to. And…you'll have to write me a song. Best friends would do that for each other, wouldn't they?"

Relieved and almost giddy with happiness, Skye nodded. "I'll write you as many you want."

"Just one." Camille came over to hug Skye. "You're pretty damn amazing."

"So are you. All of you. Thank you for not hating me."

"As if." Camille turned up the volume on the stereo a little. "Did you ever write anything for Cameron?"

"No." Skye bit her lip. She was back to cloaking the truth, but Cameron's Nashville career wasn't her secret to share. It was, however, hers to keep if she expected him to keep hers. Just because Camille and her parents knew didn't mean she wanted the world to know.

\* \* \* \*

"Cam, it's your turn to vacuum. This place is filthy."

Cameron looked up to see Hunter with his hands on his hips. "I cooked yesterday, put in two loads of laundry this morning, and emptied the dishwasher less than an hour ago. How about the rest of you start earning your keep?"

"It's still your turn."

"Just like it's your turn to fuck off." Not in the mood for any more domestic shit, or brotherly shit for that matter, Cameron walked out. The house felt claustrophobic. Maeville felt claustrophobic.

"I wish you'd stop fucking running." Hunter yelled after him from the porch. Then came chasing after him.

"Go away."

Hunter grabbed Cameron's shoulder. "Stop running."

"I'm not running." Cameron yanked away. "I'm getting some air."

"I wish you'd stop lying."

It was a direct hit although Hunter didn't know it. Cameron sneered. "I wish you'd go away."

He walked faster, and Hunter fell back. After a while when he looked over his shoulder, his brother had disappeared. Cameron didn't know where he was going, so he ended up back at the house after a very cold hour.

It was getting dark, and he could smell something spicy cooking when he opened the door. Although starving, he bypassed the kitchen and ended up in his daddy's office. He'd locked away the hidden stash of alcohol so Straw couldn't get to it, and now he got out a bottle of whiskey that was probably older than him. Maybe older than his daddy.

Although aiming to get drunk, he took the time to enjoy the pleasurable burn down his throat and the pungent, slightly smoky flavor of his daddy's favorite brand. He'd barely explored the first sip before his brothers burst into the room.

"Seriously? How about a little privacy?"

"Later," Reid said, eyeing the whiskey and getting out three more glasses. "This is an intervention. We had one for Straw, now we're having one for you."

"I've had one sip."

"Not what he means," Hunter said.

Cameron looked at his brothers surrounding him, sitting on various pieces of furniture around the room each holding a crystal tumbler of amber liquid. He had no idea what the intervention was for, but if Straw had felt as cornered as he did right now, he didn't blame him for acting like he had. "What the hell is this about?"

"Your grumpy bear routine. It's getting old," Reid said. "We're all angry about something. You don't think I'd rather be watching the sunset on the way to Tobago? That Hunter would rather be free of our amateurish butting in at the mill? Or that Straw would rather be hauling in fish up river free from us telling him how to run his life? But we're all giving this a go. Even Straw has come around. Well, sorta. But then there's you, moping over your lost career and your lost love. If you don't like it here, then why don't you just leave?"

"We all have to stay," Cameron pointed out tersely.

"No, we don't. But we're choosing to." Reid sprang up and started pacing. "I don't need to stick around and coddle you and Straw out of your self-inflicted depressions. And you don't need to stick around if Nashville is so much better. None of us will die a horrible death if we don't get a quarter of the mill and of this house. Maybe we'd like to have it, but we'd survive without it. Especially because we know Hunter would take care of it. Daddy was right, he's the right man for it."

"You know," Hunter drawled. "This isn't what we agreed to say."

Reid shrugged. "So I didn't stick to the script. I was feeling inspired. Sue me."

"I just might. Cam, what Reid is so ineloquently trying to say is that maybe we can help you with whatever's weighing you down. I talked to the lawyer, and he says there's no law that says we have to be either here or at the mill every hour or every day. You can head to Nashville for shows or whatever as long as you spend the majority of your time here for one year. We can work it out."

Wishing he'd had more to drink, Cameron emptied his glass without enjoyment or respect for the age of the liquor. A war raged inside of him. His pride battling his conscience to a soundtrack of Skye's words about how he'd wasted years because of vanity and self-pity. He reached out for the whiskey bottle and poured himself a second glass.

No one said anything. Straw was swirling his drink and watching it with rapt fascination. Cameron suspected he'd been forced to take part in this little event. Reid met Cameron's gaze head on while Hunter's was flickering around the room between all of them. Cameron emptied his glass again and jumped in at the deep end.

"It's been three and a half years since I last stood on a stage. Since I last sung. I don't want or need to go back to Nashville because there's nothing for me there. I'm Cameron Madigan, not even a one-hit-wonder, as that would suggest I've had a hit. I haven't. I've had a fiasco."

"But…your album? Your success?" Reid narrowed his eyes. "Was it all a lie?"

"Not the album, but the success." Cameron sighed. "At first, when I was still writing and calling home, I made a point to tell about the gigs but not how few people were at them. I told you about the album, but not about how it barely made the charts or how few people ever bought it. Blame it on pride or whatever. When I stopped writing home, I guess…"

"We thought it was because you were too busy," Hunter finished flatly.

"Yeah. And I let you."

"What have you been doing in Nashville then?" Reid asked.

"Surviving. Brooding. Taking one crappy job after another to avoid sleeping in my car. Pretending that some day my old manager or record company would realize they'd made a mistake screwing me over. Avoiding dealing with the truth. Take your pick."

Straw snorted. "And I thought I was a fuckup."

"Straw," Hunter hissed.

"No, he's right," Cameron said. "I am a fuckup. It's not unusual to fail, but pretending it didn't happen isn't the way to deal with it. It just wasn't until I'd already started the charade that I realized how hard it was to end it. It didn't even feel like a charade until I came back home. I'm sorry I lied to you."

"So what?" Straw asked.

Reid sipped his whiskey. "You miss out on being a star, your ego takes a hit, but Straw's right—so what? If that's what you've been so grumpy about, it's time you stop. You're alive. The world's full of opportunities."

Those were not the reactions Cameron had expected. He looked at Hunter, who shrugged. "I suppose I already knew. Or at least suspected."

"How?" Cameron asked. The only person who knew—at least as far as he was aware—was Skye. Although she and Hunter were friends, he couldn't imagine her saying anything.

"Ever hear of this newfangled invention all the kids are using these days? It's called the Internet and it's full of information and pictures and stuff. Or, as in your case, suspiciously void of. If you were doing shows and interviews, I just wondered why none of it ever made it online. Your website even disappeared."

"I suppose lots of people have deduced the same as you." The thought filled Cameron with horror. All this time Hunter had just been humoring him…maybe nearly everyone had. If that was the case, perhaps hauling ass out of town wasn't such a bad idea. Inheritance be damned.

"So, now that we've established that none of us are stars and that we're just a bunch of nobodies, there's a deliciously cold dinner waiting in the kitchen. And since you didn't cook, Cam, you can do the dishes."

Reid led the way to the kitchen, Hunter and Straw following. Cameron trailed behind, more than a little shocked at the reactions, or almost lack thereof, he'd gotten. It made him wish he'd done it ages ago and felt less stupid about it. Just admitting it had his ego smarting something awful even if his brothers hadn't thought it as big a deal as he had.

* * * *

The week dragged. Skye felt her mood slipping further and further below freezing, but she didn't know how to stop it. Around her, most people were getting ready for Christmas, sending the atmosphere soaring with the festive mood Skye usually loved. But not this year. This year, Cameron Madigan was back in town and affected her in ways she couldn't afford to be affected. She didn't have the usual patience with those of the clinic's patients who really just came in to talk because they were lonely, she had none of the good ideas that normally meant that she got people in her life creative and thoughtful Christmas presents, and she had absolutely none of the energy required for a Christmas in Maeville.

Christmas in the small town William Madigan had founded more than hundred and fifty years ago wasn't just a holiday. It was an event. It was said to be because his bride, a girl who'd come all the way from Ireland to marry him, had been unusually fond of Christmas. It was she he'd named the town after, and it was she whose memory was still celebrated every year when the people of Maeville went out of their way to enrich each others' lives by giving and helping on a scale Skye hadn't heard of anywhere else.

The energy required for it was nowhere to be found inside Skye, and knowing she had to go through the motions anyway—help out at the mill every weekend, bake enough cookies and pies to feed half the town, and volunteer for at least a dozen different smaller events—was exhausting to even think about.

She wished the blame for it lay solely on Cameron, but she knew it didn't. She'd pushed the only man she'd ever loved away because of lofty ideals. Trouble was that those lofty ideals were very precious to her, and as much as she loved him, she truly believed he had to accept the realities before he could properly move ahead with his life. And a man who lived a lie had accepted nothing.

Skye sighed and looked at the computer screen for a moment. Then she rose and plastered on the most sincere smile she could muster. It wasn't very impressive, but it would have to do. "Mr. Hamilton, you can go in to see the doctor now. And Andrea, if you'll follow me."

Andrea, a high school student who lived next to Skye's parents, was a chatterer. Skye tried to keep up with the stream of information about boys, bands, and BFFs while administering the blood test the girl's scheduled diabetes checkups required.

"That Cameron Madigan is looking mighty delish. You used to date him, didn't you? Like ages ago?"

Skye labeled the vial. "Yes, I did. Ages ago."

"I wonder why he came back." Andrea swung her feet from the examination table. "Well, why he's staying that is. His daddy's funeral was weeks ago. Do you know why he hasn't gone back to Nashville?"

"Maybe he realized what a delightful place Maeville is," Skye suggested, not about to discuss the Madigans' family business.

"Oh my Lord, I cannot wait to leave. Nothing ever happens here," Andrea whined. "I'm gonna go to New York for college. Or maybe California. I haven't decided yet. Chris, you know my boyfriend, right? Well, he wants me to go with him to Seattle. But I told him it's way too cold up there."

"New York can be plenty cold," Skye pointed out, part amused, part ready to send the girl on her way.

"I know, but it's New York." Andrea sighed delightedly. "It would just be so awesome."

Smiling, Skye finished the checkup on autopilot. She remembered what it was like to be young like Andrea and full of romantic, unrealistic dreams. Skye still felt young, but she'd at least gotten enough experience to know realistic from unrealistic. Realistic dreams shouldn't be dreams—they should be plans. And as soon as the workday was over, her plans included baking pies enough to feed half the town. She wasn't going to let Cameron ruin any more of her dreams, and Christmas was something she sometimes found herself dreaming of at all times of the year.

# Chapter Twenty

A week before Christmas, Skye let Camille drag her out on a Saturday night. It was just down to the local bar, but Skye had been keeping busy with work and everything else she could find to fill her time. It was just easier that way, with less time to think and analyze the path life had taken her down since...no, she wasn't even going to think his name, not tonight, she promised herself in her head as she sipped her beer and looked around the crowded bar. It wasn't usually this busy, but she figured people needed a little break from their Christmas preparations.

Half of Maeville was there. At least that's how it seemed. And if Skye looked around more than once, it wasn't to look for...him. Though, it was a little strange that he wasn't there since Hunter, Reid, and Julian were all sitting across from her around the table, where she and Camille were filling up one side with Wendy and Sam. Maybe he was sick. And if he was, he'd be stubborn enough not to come down to the clinic even if it was serious. Just to avoid her. And who could blame him after the way she'd rejected him? Rejected the love of her life. Skye pushed the thoughts away and refilled her glass from the beer pitcher as she struggled to tune back in on the conversation around her.

"But the seasoned softwood can't have a moisture content of more than nineteen percent, so we have to," Hunter said.

Of course they were talking shop.

Skye tuned them back out. She and Wendy were the only ones at the table not working at the mill, and Wendy was so crazy in love with Sam that she had no difficulties getting interested in his job. Skye knew the feeling well. She'd once been as interested in sawmill business as anyone at the table with her.

Perhaps she should just head home. She'd made an appearance, but she wasn't good company for anyone. She couldn't even fake it, which was clear from the weird looks she kept getting from the Madigan brothers. Perhaps they knew that she'd sent Cameron packing.

Skye winced. She'd promised herself not even to think his name tonight, and she'd been doing so well for — she looked at her watch — almost forty minutes. Sighing, she gave up. She couldn't keep Cameron out of her mind anymore than she could keep him out of her heart or her life. They were fated. It was that simple.

It hit her then, while sipping beer and half-listening to a semi-decent band on the small stage in the corner, that she'd missed something vital in her reasoning and internal analyzes. Cameron wasn't the only one who needed to accept realities. Sure, he had to face up to the fact that his life hadn't turned out the way he'd dreamed it would and take responsibility for it.

But so did she.

Cameron wasn't the star-to-be he'd once been. He was a man who'd been burned, been disappointed, and been let down. By others and by himself. And, she saw now, by her. Where was her understanding? Where was her support? She'd failed him in Nashville just as he'd failed himself.

Anytime during the years she'd known about his lack of music career, she could have thrown him a bone. One song penned by herself and André, and he would have been able to revive his dream. So why hadn't she done that? Petty vengeance, she admitted. He'd left her to her own devices, so she'd done the same as soon as she'd gotten the chance.

And now he was back. More mature, more cautious, more honest. Because he might be lying to the world, but he'd showed her real, naked honesty as far as his feelings were concerned.

And she hadn't accepted this new, mature Cameron. She still saw him as the humiliated failure who wouldn't admit to it. Yet, the last time they'd seen each other, he'd admitted to the most important thing. That he wanted a future for them.

Skye wasn't even aware that she'd stood up before the chair hit the floor behind her. "I have to go."

Hunter rose, too, and came around to her side of the table. "Are you okay?"

"Yeah, I just…I have to go."

Reaching for her coat, she looked up when Hunter put his hand on her arm. "I really wish you'd stay."

"I can't, Hunter. I have to talk to Cam I just realized something important that he needs to know."

"He isn't home. Wait until the morning." He bent to pick up her chair. "Have another drink."

"Where is he?" Skye suddenly felt a desperate need to make things right with Cameron. And it couldn't wait.

"I can't tell you, I'm sorry. Please just trust me and sit back down."

The imploring look in his eyes made her sit down although she wasn't entirely sure why. Then she happened to look at the others at the table, who were staring oddly at her.

"Are you okay?" Camille asked her.

"Yes, I'm fine." As desperate as she'd been before, now she just felt helpless and awkward. "I'm sorry."

To avoid the curious looks, she kept her head down until the talk picked back up. Then she leaned across the table toward Hunter. "What's going on?"

"Just trust me please," Hunter said again, then smiled as he reached over to squeeze her hand briefly. "Stay another half hour, and if you still want to go home then, I'll take you myself."

It was mostly curiousness that kept Skye seated at the table. Hunter knew something, something that had to do with Cameron, and whether it was because Hunter knew Cameron was coming later or because he knew his brother was out on a date or something, Skye decided that she could trust Hunter's judgment. Besides, if Cameron really wasn't home, sitting at the bar waiting beat going out in the cold night to look for him.

* * * *

If this wasn't proof that women made men crazy, Cameron didn't know what it was. Well, besides utter madness. He paced the small hallway and went over the words in his head. He'd been temporarily insane when he'd hatched the idea and then been thoroughly goaded by his brothers. And everyone knew what happened when a guy was goaded by his brothers. Wars and revolutions had probably started that way.

It might have sounded good in theory. Smooth, even. But out here in the real world where Cameron was feeling the cold and remembering the last time he'd been in a slightly similar situation, things never went smoothly. At least not in his life. He'd probably just make a fool of himself and mess things up even further than they already were.

When Reid appeared, Cameron nearly jumped a mile.

"Easy there. You ready?"

"No. This was a stupid idea."

Snorting, Reid patted Cameron on the shoulder. "Yep. But that's the way it has to be when women are involved. If you haven't gotten that yet, I'm not sure you should go through with this thing."

"Me neither," Cameron muttered, knowing that of course he would go through with it. If making a fool of himself in front of half of the town would help his cause, then that's what he'd do. With a goddamn smile on his face.

"You remember how to use that thing?" Reid asked, nodding toward the guitar leaning against the wall.

"I've been practicing."

"Good boy. Did you wash behind your ears?"

Cameron laughed. "Go away."

Saluting, Reid did just that, throwing a, "Break a leg!" over his shoulder.

Cameron wouldn't be the least bit surprised if that ended up being the result of the night. A broken leg. He looked at his watch. Five minutes till show time.

Rob stuck his head in. "You ready?"

"Not really," Cameron replied. "But what the hell. Let's do this thing."

Rob grinned. "That's the spirit."

Rob had been extremely understanding when Cameron approached him with his plan. And then he'd gotten excited. Cameron might have admitted to not being the star everyone thought he was, but he'd played and sung enough locally in his youth that people still remembered that he had talent. So without reservation, Rob had given him a Saturday night slot and permission to carry out his performance the way he wanted to.

Now Cameron just had to pull it off. Picking up the guitar, he went down the hallway and peered out of the door leading into the bar. He'd looked before, so he knew where to find who he was looking for. His brothers, Camille…and Skye. She looked like she was in a world of her own. Sipping her beer, staring as if seeing nothing, and looking sorely out of place in a room where people were talking, laughing, and having a good time. He felt her pain but was grateful she was there.

He took a deep breath when Rob went onto the small stage and grabbed the microphone. The nerves were threatening to make him physically ill. He'd done this so many times he couldn't even count them, but that was years ago. And it had never mattered as much as it did tonight.

"Ladies and gentlemen, may I have your attention please?" Rob grinned and waited until people quieted down a little. "I have a special surprise for you tonight. Y'all know him, so please give a warm welcome to Maeville's very own Cameron Madigan!"

There was a moment of terror when the bar turned completely quiet. Or at least that's how it seemed to Cameron, who was seriously considering making a run for it. Then he heard something he hadn't heard in a long, long time. Applause. Applause meant for him. He put one foot in front of the other, plastered the most sincere smile his nerves would permit on his face, and walked onto the stage. It was now or never if he wanted to make his dream come true.

* * * *

Skye felt a small, painful snap in her neck when her head whipped up at the mention of Cameron's name. It couldn't be… Surely he wasn't going to…but he was. Skye's fingernails bit painfully into her palms as she watched the slightly shaky smile on Cameron's face as he quickly glanced around. Then strummed his guitar and started playing. It was the song he'd had engraved on the necklace she wore around her neck. Involuntarily, her hand reached up to clutch it.

When he started singing, she could hear the tremors in his voice. Did anyone else know what it was he was doing? Blinking away tears and with her gaze locked on him, she heard his voice steadying and his confidence growing. He was finding himself, maybe even healing himself, and he was allowing her, along with a lot of other people who'd known him all his life, to witness the transformation.

The years of disuse had done nothing to hurt his voice. It washed over her the same way a whispered caress did and melted something inside of her that was only his to touch.

As he stood there, on a small stage in a small town bar wearing a pair of worn jeans and his preferred plaid shirt, looking as though he belonged in the spotlight, it was hard to believe Nashville hadn't been all over him.

The song ended, and the applause was deafening. So Nashville hadn't wanted him, but Maeville definitely loved their star. Cameron chuckled into the microphone. The sound made Skye shiver. She glanced across the table and saw all three Madigans grin. Reid gave her a thumbs up that made her wonder if they also knew exactly how special the performance was. Then Cameron spoke, and she turned her head to look at him.

"Thank you. I appreciate it more than you know."

The applause died down.

"Truthfully, I'd planned to say something before the first song, but the nerves got to me, so I stuck with what I knew. I always was better at singing than talking, but if you'll indulge me for a minute, I'd like to say something."

His eyes sought out the table Skye was sitting at, and he smiled softly before continuing. "I guess y'all know I went over to Nashville. Made myself an album and got to stand on some of the stages I'd been dreaming of. But that's where the dream ended. I wasn't good enough to really make a name for myself."

Skye felt as if her heart had stopped beating in her chest. When he went all out, he sure as hell went all out.

"It took a while to accept, which is why I never did much to correct folks from back home when they went ahead and assumed I was still singing and doing well at it, too. When y'all thought I was living the good life doing what I'd always dreamed of, I was really serving beer and cleaning bathrooms. And I'm sorry for not making that clear. It hurts to have a dream ripped away from you.

"So why tell you now, and why tell you like this, you ask? Well, when I found out I wasn't good enough, I vowed never to stand on a stage or ever sing again. Never play the guitar my momma left me when she passed, and never to listen to music unless I couldn't avoid it. I kept that promise to myself for years, but then something happened that I figure happens to a lot of men. A woman happened."

Whistles and supportive yells made Cameron laugh. Skye knew Maeville, and Maeville knew people's business, so when she glanced around, she saw a lot of people looking at her. So he wasn't just putting himself in the spotlight, he was hauling her halfway into it as well. Her cheeks felt hot, but her attention returned to the stage and the man on it.

"Glad I'm not the only one. But the bottom line is that I'm proving a point to her tonight. See, she thinks I gave up music because my dream died. That's not the whole truth, however. My dream lives, and music is bound to it, so I'm reclaiming it tonight. Not in Nashville, but in Maeville. I'm right where I want to be. And by the time I walk off this stage, hopefully I'll have proven that I'm a man worth marrying."

Whistles and catcalls made Skye almost deaf. Then they died down as Cameron started playing his guitar again. Had he just said what she thought he'd said? The song was unfamiliar, and Skye's mind was so much in an uproar that she only caught bits and pieces of the lyrics although she tried to hang onto his every word.

"That was *Tell It True*," Cameron said when the song ended and he'd put his guitar down. "I haven't written many songs, but I was feeling inspired. And Skye, I felt a new song was the least I could give you when I have to admit that the ring I'm offering you is an old one that I've carried with me for more than six years."

Skye didn't know if the room had quieted down or if it was just the sound of the blood rushing to her head that blocked out all other sounds. But it was quiet enough to hear a pin drop as things and people faded away. Cameron was all she could see, and he walked down toward her, except it didn't seem real. It didn't seem real that... She gasped as he reached her and held out a sparkling ring with a square cut diamond and tiny music notes woven together on the band.

"You're the dream, Skye." The tremors were back in his voice.

She rose on shaky legs. Vaguely she was aware that they weren't alone, but she could only make out one face—his sexy, familiar, and beloved one. He still held out the ring, and his eyes were locked on her.

"Ask me," she prompted. She'd never known anything more clearly than that she needed Cameron Madigan to ask her the question that went with that ring. That went with the things he'd said up on that stage.

He smiled as the nerves left his face. "I don't have to. The answer is all over your face. We're getting married."

"Yes, we are," she agreed as the truth surged through her body and left her giddy and warm and thankful that there was such a thing as second chances in the world and a man like Cameron Madigan. And both were hers.

Cupping the back of her head, he fused their lips together as he one-handed tried to put the ring on her finger. She laughed even as she gave in to the kiss. Gave in to him.

He broke away and brought up her hand to look at. "Looks like it belongs there."

"Looks like," she agreed.

"I love you more than anything," he whispered to her. "You've always been the dream, Skye, and you always will be. Nothing else matters. If I need music, you can give it to me. I forgot that for a while. Just like I forgot where home is. It's here. With you."

"If you forget it again, I'm coming after you this time." She locked her hands behind his neck and pressed their foreheads together. "I love you, and you're mine now."

The kiss was long, hot, messy, and slightly inappropriate for the public venue. When they broke apart for air, the crowd surrounding them cheered. Skye had almost forgotten they were there.

As she was being passed around for hugs, she heard Rob speak from the stage. "Not quite what I had expected, Cam, but you're welcome back on my stage anytime. With or without the show. Congrats, y'all."

Cameron and Skye locked gazes, him being slapped on the back by Reid and Julian, and her being hugged by Camille. The brilliancy of the smile on his face made her certain that he was right where he was supposed to be. And so was she. Well, almost. Bypassing a couple of people she barely knew but who'd apparently gotten caught up in the mood, she found her way into Cameron's arms. He squeezed her and kissed the top of her head. Now they were both where they were supposed to be.

**The End**

### Dear Reader

Thank you visiting Maeville and the Madigans — I hope you enjoyed Skye and Cameron's story. Please consider leaving a review on the site you purchased the book or on Goodreads. It would truly mean the world to me. Beneath you will see how to contact and follow me on social media — don't be a stranger! Sign up and follow me so you'll know when the next Madigan River book is out. Camille and Hunter are up next. And if you keep turning the pages, you can check out the first chapter right now. Enjoy!

### All my love, Jannie

### Contact Jannie

Website: www.jannielund.com

Newsletter: www.jannielund.com/mailinglist-signup

Twitter: @jannielund

Facebook: www.facebook.com/jannielundwriter

## About Jannie

Since she was old enough to put words on paper, Jannie has been writing, and since 2008, she's been fortunate enough to have those words published once in a while. She writes in English and Danish. When she's not making up fictional worlds, she enjoys a wide array of other creative pastimes such as yarn dyeing, crochet, knitting, needle felting, and sewing. You might also spot her at the nearest beach with a camera and a notebook, hunting for her next idea.


## Available Now

MORELLO COVE SERIES
1 – Vintage Dreams
2 – Dreams of Home
3 – Dreaming With You

STAND ALONES
A Thousand Sunsets
Finding Clara
Clear as Glass

# Excerpt from TELL ME A SECRET
# (MADIGAN RIVER BOOK 2)

# Chapter One

As much as Camille loved the busy, noisy days at the Madigan's sawmill, there was something to be said for getting some work done during the quiet days when no one else was around. Like on New Years Eve Day when everyone else was busy preparing to see the New Year in with a level of fuss it hadn't had time to deserve yet. She didn't understand the need. There was every chance, if she got really caught up in her work, that she'd work through the time when one year became the next. It wouldn't be the first time.

She sipped her coffee and added another invoice to the neatly formed stack to her right. It wasn't as if her work was her entire life. Not really. She just liked it. Liked being part of something bigger than herself and liked that others were dependent on her doing her job. It made a person feel less lonely. If Thomas Madigan had known that when he offered her a job a decade earlier was doubtful, but he'd likely saved her sanity by giving a lost high school student a chance.

Camille still missed him. She knew people in Maeville had seen very little in Thomas Madigan to miss, but they'd been alike in some ways and that had mattered to her, since she'd never seen herself mirrored in others enough for it to become something to dismiss.

Like her, he'd rewarded loyalty with trust and trust with loyalty. Though, both had been hard earned with him. Camille had respected that. And no matter what anyone had thought of him, and people had thought and said plenty about the brusque great-great-grandchild of the town's founder, his death had left a void.

A missing report quickly shifted Camille's thoughts from tender ones about Thomas Madigan to less tender ones about his son. "Dammit, Hunter," she muttered as she searched for the missing papers. He'd promised to leave it on her desk before going home the other night. Of all the frustrating men in the world, Hunter Madigan was surely the worst.

Annoyed, she grabbed the phone and dialed his number. A cough greeted her when he picked up, because of course he was too frustrating to just say hello like a normal person.

"Hello to you, too."

"Camille?"

Hunter was her boss. He was her friend. He was someone she could easily fall in love with if she let herself, and by God she wanted to sometimes. This was not one of those times. In fact, right then she had to remind herself that he had the power to make her jobless. He wouldn't do that, of course—he might be frustrating, but he wasn't plain dumb. The sawmill would fall to pieces without her, especially now that all four Madigan brothers were trying to run it together. If they agreed what to have for breakfast by nightfall, it had been a good day. Corralling them to come together about the mill was a fulltime job, which was one of the reasons she was spending New Years Eve Day doing paperwork.

"That's right. You sound a bit rough. Did I catch you at a bad time?"

He coughed again. "No. Ah, just not feeling well. Something wrong?"

Camille swallowed a sigh. Hunter almost always asked her that whenever she called him, as if the only reason she could possibly have for wanting to talk to him was if she had a problem she needed him to solve. Men. Although…he was right this time. "Remember the inventory report supposed to be on my desk?"

"Um…"

"Let me help you out. It's not here."

"You're at the mill now? Jesus, Camille. It's New Years Eve."

"That doesn't change the fact that the report isn't where you said it would be. So where is it?"

"I have absolutely no idea. I can't think when I'm dying."

"The flu?" Camille guessed. It was going around, she knew from Skye, her best friend and trained nurse.

"At least."

Although Hunter was the most humble, down-to-earth, no-fuss kind of man Camille had ever known, it came as no surprise that he was as big of a baby about being sick as everyone else of the male persuasion. She couldn't remember him really being sick before, though, so she supposed he could make a fuss if he wanted to.

"Drink some orange juice and have Reid or Julian make you some soup."

"They're sick, too."

Camille closed her eyes briefly, imaging the misery in the big house on Madigan Avenue. Lord help anyone who stepped a foot in that house.

For Skye's sake, she hoped the fourth Madigan brother wasn't sick, too, or she and Cameron would have a miserable time in the romantic little inn up the coast where they were seeing in the New Year and belatedly celebrating their engagement.

"Poor boys. I'll let you get back to bed and just work around the report. Happy New Year, Hunter." Even as she spoke, she saw the decision forming in her mind, half against her will.

"Yeah, you too."

The last thing she heard was another cough, and she hung up with a sigh. Damn him. There was no question that he was being a baby about having the flu or whatever. But there was also no question that he wasn't faking the whole thing. And men couldn't help it, could they? Camille gathered the papers on her desk into neat stacks and rose from her chair. She could work tomorrow. It wasn't like she'd be suffering from a hangover or anything.

After closing up, she went outside. The sun was shining, but the wind was cold, and she wrapped the jacket closer around her as she walked to her car. The mill was her second home, and she loved it equally when it was busy and full of noise as when it was quiet like now. Memories from over the years floated around in the air along with the smell of freshly cut wood. Stopping for a moment, she took it all in. Then she realized that she was about to brave the grocery store just a few short hours shy of New Years Eve. Lord help her.

* * * *

"Make him stop," Reid begged, appearing in the door to Hunter's room.

"You make him stop," Hunter grumbled, trying to ignore the sound of Straw retching in the bathroom. What did a man have to do to die in peace around here? "Or just close the door. You're the one standing."

Reid shuffled off, and Hunter went back to being miserable on his own. Except…not as much on his own as he would have liked. At least once a day he wished for his solitary cabin up river where anyone rarely bothered him and generally let him tango with death in peace. His brothers thought they'd gotten the brunt of the forceful blow their daddy had delivered them in the form of his last will and testament, which had demanded that they all live and work together for a year in order for them to receive their inheritance. If just one of them left, Hunter would inherit everything. So they pitied themselves from time to time about having to give up their lives. None of them considered what Hunter had had to give up. His solitude, for one, which he'd prized above almost all else. He'd also been the only one without a choice. The will said nothing about what would happen to the house and the business if Hunter decided to split. Not that he would, which his daddy had known, but it still left him feeling trussed up, tied to a fate that wasn't his own for a year.

He groaned and turned over in his bed. He was sweaty and felt gross whereas just moments before he'd been chilled to the bone. Everything ached, and it wasn't that long ago that he had been the one retching in the bathroom. He should write down his will himself. Leave his headaches and troubles to his brothers. Maybe even his flu.

With a mouth resembling sandpaper, he dragged himself out of bed to go find something to drink. The retching in the bathroom had stopped, but either Reid or Straw were moaning and emitting all kinds of pathetic sounds somewhere. Hunter wondered if Cam was sick, too, ruining his romantic getaway with Skye. Then decided it would only be fair if he was. Just because he'd gotten his girl didn't mean he should start feeling special.

Halfway down the stairs, he heard the doorbell. Great. Company. That was exactly what he needed. Reid felt differently and appeared from the living room and heading for the door, not seeming to care that none of them were properly dressed or in the mood for guests.

"Please tell me you've come to shoot me," Reid said as he opened the door. "Camille. Thank heavens. You'll put me out of my misery, right? I'm dying."

"Yeah, you look it," she agreed and pushed past him, impressively carrying three grocery bags. She looked up the stairs at Hunter. "Hi, you look like crap."

Hunter ran a hand through his hair, resisting the urge to wipe his hand on his rumpled T-shirt. "Thanks." He could always count on Camille not to sugarcoat things. It was part of what he liked so much about her.

"No problem." Camille went into the kitchen, leaving Hunter and Reid to look at each other and shrug. Camille was a quiet force of nature Hunter had yet to figure out how to stop from doing exactly what she wanted, and he was certainly no match for her in his current state.

If she wanted to take pity on them—and she often did whether they wanted her to or not—she was damn well going to take pity on them. He followed her into the kitchen while Reid returned to the living room, where he'd most likely claimed the couch.

Camille was emptying grocery bags. "Heaven knows why I'm bothering with you slobs."

"I'm wondering that, too," Hunter admitted, looking around and trying to see the kitchen through her eyes. It was a mess. The whole house was, in fact, including its residents. Exhausted from standing more than two minutes, Hunter sank down on a chair. "You should just leave us to our misery."

"I probably should." Camille met his gaze, and the hint of a smile appeared on her lips. She had such pretty ones, never slathered in unnatural colors or sticky, shiny stuff.

"But you won't." Hunter said. It wasn't a bold or cocky remark. It was just the truth as he knew it. Camille had the biggest, most beautiful heart in the world. She was fiercely loyal, unpredictable, and a tempting riddle Hunter often wondered if he was man enough to solve.

"No."

He watched her silently for a while, distracted from his misery by the grace always present in her, from the tip of her toes to the top of her head. She was like a dancer, full of fluid movements, even in a messy, unfamiliar kitchen, where she was busy emptying grocery bags and clearing counter tops.

"Stop staring, it's creepy. Go back to bed, or better yet—go take a shower. You smell."

Okay, so it was mostly her movements that were graceful. What came out of her mouth wasn't always, but you could trust it to be honest. And if she could smell him all the way over there…well, he just might have to delay his imminent death a little longer and haul himself into the shower for a minute or two. Maybe he'd get lucky and drown.

\* \* \* \*

Camille allowed herself to watch Hunter leave the kitchen. Then she sighed and started making soup. If she didn't keep busy, there was a big risk that she'd end up standing around mooning like a love-struck teenager. And that just wouldn't do.

Once the soup was simmering, she cleaned up the kitchen. It was clear no one had bothered to lately. From there she continued on to the other rooms, checking the soup from time to time. Reid was snoring on the couch in the living room, so she decided to go upstairs to change his sheets and air out his bedroom. Once she'd done that, she did the same in Hunter's, as he was also absent from the bed it looked like he'd been living in for some time. Boys were so gross sometimes. Grown boys, too.

She wondered what it was like to go from having lived alone for years to having to bunk with your brothers all over again. From what she knew, it was far from easy. Julian tested everyone's patience with his sour attitude, anger, and tendency to turn to alcohol. Half the time, Reid looked like someone who was on his way out of town, no doubt itching to be back on his boat and sailing wherever he pleased.

Cameron had perplexed her when he'd first returned, as she expected he had most people. The tasty morsel of a secret he'd been hiding had explained perfectly why the Nashville music star they'd all thought him to be had been content to return to his small-town home and work at his family's sawmill. He'd never been a star. He'd been a failure. Personally, Camille didn't think less of him for that. Quite the opposite, in fact. If you didn't test your wings, you'd never know if they could carry you. And it was the testing that took guts, not the actual flying.

And then there was Hunter. A lot of things in Camille's life circled back to Hunter Madigan and had for a lot longer than she cared to admit. But that was beside the point. He was a private, quiet man, and she could only imagine how he felt having to live with three loud brothers right there on Madigan Avenue. There was a lot of responsibility on his shoulders, what with keeping them all in check at home and at the sawmill. On paper, they were equals, but in reality, Hunter was the boss.

A cough behind her made her twirl around. Hunter stood in the doorway, wearing a towel around his waist and nothing else. Well, that was a lie. Drops of water clung to his neck and chest, dripping from his hair. He was a sight to behold dry with his wavy dark blonde hair that was always a smidgen too long, intense gray eyes, and a body that showcased what manual labor could do for a man. But wet…Camille swallowed with some difficulty, mouth suddenly dry as a desert.

"Stop staring, it's creepy," Hunter said, echoing her own words back to her. He grinned, though, looking like the long shower had done him some good. Maybe he was off the critical list. Or maybe he liked being ogled blatantly. Camille had never thought of herself as a blatant ogler, but there she was—unable to take her eyes off him.

"Want to stay for the rest of the show or do you mind if I get dressed in private?"

Camille put down the pillow she'd been holding. "Of course not."

His chuckle followed her out. Damn the man.

Out in the hallway, she took a deep breath. Hunter was not supposed to get to her. She'd allowed it once, and it wasn't happening again. Back in the fall, he'd asked here out. It hadn't been out of blue exactly. She supposed there had been flirting happening for a while before that, but in a way she'd never expected anything to come of it.

As it turned out, nothing had come of it. Before she'd had a chance to answer him, someone out at the mill had interrupted them, and later that day Hunter had found his daddy dead, pushing thoughts of dates firmly in the background for both of them. Since, the grief had lessened, but Hunter had never asked again. And Camille had promised herself to do the best she could not to think about it.

Going back downstairs, she put in a load of laundry before checking the soup again. She'd bake some bread and maybe a cake of some kind. She'd brought the basics over, so it all depended on what she could find in the cupboards.

"What are you doing here?" Julian shuffled into the kitchen, looking more pathetic than Hunter and Reid put together. How anyone, least of all his sorry excuse of a momma, could take one look at his angelic face and not want to mother him was beyond her. Of course, that angelic face was more often than not set in a scowl or a sneer. And often the storm in the gray eyes was glassy from too much alcohol or drugs. He was such a beautiful boy—and that was a lie since he was most definitely a young man—but he did his best to hide it.

"Making you soup."

He considered that. "Do Hunter and Reid get any?"

"Weren't you taught to share as a child?"

"Sure. I was also taught to mind my manners in front of company, to say my prayers every night, and that nothing was more important than your last name. That doesn't mean I live by it today." He went to the fridge and grabbed the orange juice she'd bought. When he appeared to be about to drink from the carton, she cleared her throat sharply. He grinned weakly and reached for a glass.

Camille had adored Julian's daddy, respected him, admired him, loved him. However, she hadn't been blind to his faults, and one of them had been in how he'd treated his sons. He'd mostly raised them alone, having had very little luck with love. The four Madigan brothers had four different mothers, three of them who'd had the title of Mrs. Madigan, and the fourth too flighty for marriage.

The relationships had been brief, and the result had been very little maternal influence on the boys. Cameron's momma had died during childbirth, Hunter's not suited for small-town life, Reid's had the same adventurous gene as her son, and Julian's was just the worst woman in the history of women. She'd plain rejected her son, only resurfacing from time to time to manipulate the Madigans for money.

It wasn't so strange that Camille saw a kindred spirit in Julian. One rejected child recognized another. Saw through the façade put in place to hide the pain.

# Excerpt from VINTAGE DREAMS
# (MORELLO COVE 1)

# **Chapter One**

Danielle fussed with the delicate, cream lace and took a step back to let her critical eyes take in the dress she'd been up half the night finishing. Not that there'd been any rush to get it done, but whenever one of the dresses she created started to take form, she felt a burning need to see it complete and on display at the boutique. Adding the turquoise and mother of pearl necklace completed the vision, and she took another step back. A smile bloomed on her face and satisfaction spread in her body. The dress looked exactly like she'd envisioned when she'd first put pen to paper, and that exact moment was her favorite in the whole process.

"Fleur! Come look at how awesome we are."

Danielle's best friend, business partner, and sister in all but blood came out from the back a moment later. She looked in a bit of a daze, which meant Danielle had interrupted her work. She almost felt bad, but then she looked back at the perfect vision of romance and dreams her dress and Fleur's jewelry made. Fleur would forgive her the interruption.

"What?" Fleur was usually the picture of gentleness and patience, but she became mama bear when someone got between her and her work.

"Look," Danielle just said.

Fleur looked, and Danielle watched the sun rise after a stormy night on her friend's face. The annoyance gave way to awe and pleasure. "Wow. We did good, Dani."

"We did better than good, honey. We did amazing." Danielle slung her arm around Fleur's shoulders and kissed her cheek.

Danielle and Fleur had been fourteen the first time they'd created something together. Danielle had altered a thrift store dress with her grandmother's old sewing machine and a few yards of lace, and Fleur had made a necklace for it out of lace scraps and pearl beads. They'd been prouder than peacocks, and from that moment their future had been decided. They had worked hard to learn and to save money, and the result was Annata, the boutique they'd opened on the boardwalk of their hometown of Morello Cove in Monterey Bay. Initially, they'd discussed if it was the right location to sell pricey vintage dresses and handmade jewelry that matched, but they had decided against moving the operation to the city. A wise decision, it had turned out. Women traveled far for the right outfit, and after two years Annata was a definitive success.

"It looks like a dream, doesn't it? A romantic dream full of moonlight and dancing without music." Fleur sighed happily.

Danielle squeezed her shoulder. "I'd have said that it's a piece of art, but your description sounds better. What are you working on this morning?"

"The black garnet pieces for the burgundy satin dress. And the sunrise this morning inspired me so much that I sketched two different wedding sets. Not sure why I see them as wedding sets, but I do. I'll show you later."

"I can't wait." Danielle looked at her watch. "All right, go hide in your cave. We open in ten minutes, and Susan and Trish will be here any minute."

"All right. Call me of you need me."

Danielle nodded, knowing she wouldn't. There would have to be a code red crisis of epic proportions before she called Fleur out to assist with the customers. Fleur hated it, preferring to hide in her little workshop in the back. She wasn't even comfortable coming out to say hello to customers who wanted to meet the woman behind the stunning jewelry they bought.

Fleur tolerated it, but only barely. Danielle spent as much time with the customers as she did making her dresses. She'd trained Susan and Trish, their two employees, herself, and they were equally at ease with the customers as they were carrying out Danielle's strict orders beading skirts or stitching hems. They were absolute gems.

When they arrived a few moments later, Danielle spent a few minutes going over the plans for the day with them. Weekday mornings were usually pretty slow, so she sent both Susan and Trish out back. Trish was helping her with a wedding dress that had a train with an unbearable amount of glass beads, each one stitched on by hand. Danielle couldn't wait to see it finished.

Fleur had created a diadem that resembled a crown of light when its gems sparkled, and Danielle almost envied the yet unknown bride who would wear it. Susan was asked to deal with the fabrics that had come in earlier that morning, so Danielle had the front of the boutique to herself. This meant that she fussed, corrected a lace collar here, an earring there, and made sure that every dress and every piece of jewelry shone in its own right.

The bell above the door jingling put a smile to her face. As much as she loved creating, finding the right body for her own and Fleur's creations was exciting, too. When she looked up, the body in the door opening was not *ever* going to fit into one of her dresses, however. Tall, dark, and handsome came to mind, although that did not do the man justice. Tall, yes. Dark, yes. Handsome, no. More than handsome. Sexy. Devastatingly so. The short, black hair and the icy blue eyes was a stunning combination. The black slacks and white shirt was not enough to hide the muscles beneath, and when he smiled at her, a dimple emerged on the left side of his mouth. She fought the urge to sigh dreamily like Fleur so often did in the presence of real beauty.

Danielle, puzzled at the quivering sensation the stranger invoked in her, pulled herself together and smiled welcoming. If this guy was considerate enough to buy his wife or girlfriend a handmade dress and handmade jewelry, he was pretty much perfect in her opinion. And he hadn't even opened his mouth yet.

* * *

It was with less reluctance than expected that Scott Sullivan unfolded himself from his car, gave his legs a much-needed stretch, and breathed in the fresh, clean sea air. It had been years since he'd last made the drive up to Morello Cove, and there had been as many unpleasant memories associated with driving into town as he'd been expected. However, he'd been surprised to find a few pleasant ones in the mix, as well.

Things looked as much the same as they did different. The stunning view from the boardwalk was the same, and Scott let his eyes rest on the loveliness of it for a minute. Then he looked around, seeing that Dot Maguire still sold groceries in the north end of the boardwalk. Her storefront hadn't changed in at least thirty years, and it looked sorely out of place now. It hadn't when Scott was a boy, and the boardwalk had been a place of video stores, the hardware store, a beauty parlor, and the Greek family he couldn't recall the name of who'd had that little restaurant. Now all those were gone, replaced with tourist shops, boutiques, and trendy little cafes and restaurants. He knew all this from his research, and he'd thought there'd be little charm left. But he was wrong. The town oozed charm. So much that he nearly forgot his unpleasant memories for a second.

His eyes zoomed in on a charming boutique opposite the path down to the long, thin quay that few people passing through town could resist walking out on. It was pretty in the sunshine and spectacular in a storm where it made you feel you were part of the waves, the wind, and nature in general.

The boutique sold handmade vintage dresses and jewelry, was owned by two locals, and had the best location in Morello Cove. Scott was there to secure it for his client, a fast-growing chain of coffee shops that sprouted up everywhere.

Seeing no reason to put things off and having to stay longer than necessary, he locked the car and strolled toward the boutique. There had been an antique store there before. An old woman he couldn't remember the name of had owned it, and Scott had never seen a single customer in there. Back then it had been dark and crowded with too much merchandise. Now he looked through the large windows and saw a light, airy, and...he pondered the right word as he took in the pretty, old-fashioned dresses. Romantic. That's what it was. Full of flowers, lace, and pretty things. Real pretty. There was no doubt the owners knew what they were doing, which might not work to his advantage. He'd have preferred owners in financial troubles who'd be relieved to take what he was offering.

Noting that the boutique was open, he stepped inside the door but stopped when he noticed a woman standing up. She'd been bent over a display, bent just the right way for him to get a generous glimpse of well-shaped legs and curves a man could spend a long time appreciating. A very long time. Then he saw her face, a smile lighting it up. His own smile faltered a moment. This was no mere woman. He was looking at a goddess. A curvy, sultry goddess with shiny, black curls, a mouth made for kissing, and eyes that he'd swear had gold flecks in them.

"Good morning. How can I help you?"

Scott swallowed. He'd bet his car that none of the ways he imagined her helping him was what she had in mind. He had to remind himself to be professional. He had a job to do. "Good morning. I'm looking for the owners of this place. Danielle Harris or Fleur Walker. Are either of them here?"

"I'm Danielle Harris."

Of course she was, he thought, realizing he'd expected to be charming middle-aged ladies. Not young goddesses. "Scott Sullivan," he introduced himself, offering his hand. "I'm a lawyer and representing The Java Bean Shack. I'm hoping you and Miss Walker might give me a moment of your time whenever you're both available."

Gold-flecked eyes narrowed slightly although the professional smile stayed in place. Apparently this particular goddess belonged to the race who did not like lawyers much. "What is this about?"

"The Java Bean Shack...you might have heard of them? Real popular coffee shop chain wh—"

"This isn't the boonies. I know The Java Bean Shack," she interrupted. "What do they want with us?"

Italian, Scott decided, suppressing a smile. The coloring and the temper, it all fit. "They are very interested in acquiring this location, Miss Harris. They've sent me to negotiate, and I can assure you that you will be well compensated."

"Not interested." Danielle's smile disappeared completely. "One of the seafood restaurants further down closed a while back. The place is for sale, so your coffee chain can buy that. If that's all?"

"I wish you would give me a chance to present the offer to you and your partner." Scott thought the fire in her eyes fascinating even if it did make his job a lot harder.

"I speak for us both when I say that we're not interested no matter how much money you throw at us."

Two women came into the boutique, and Danielle's professional smile returned. "Thanks for stopping by, Mr. Sullivan. Have a nice day." Dismissing him, she turned her attention to her customers.

"I'll see you later, Miss Harris." Scott grinned when she offered him a quick glare. He decided not to press the issue in front of her customers, however, and walked outside. He needed to regroup and come up with a strategy for the battle ahead. Then he sighed. As much as he'd enjoy dealing with the wonder of a woman he'd just met, it also meant that he had to resign himself to stay in town for a while. He'd packed a bag for just that purpose, but he'd spent the entire drive hoping he wouldn't need it.

Scott checked in with his clients, leaving out the particulars of his initial meeting with one of the owners, and just told them that he'd need a few days to get a chance to present the offer. Which was the truth. Danielle Harris had never given him the chance to have his say, and he intended to have it one way or the other. Then he found a nice, little hotel that had a vacant room with an ocean view and a mini bar. It was all he needed. He changed out of his slacks and dress shirt, opting for a more casual look of jeans and a t-shirt so he'd fit better in with the tourists.

Part of his plan was to intensify his research. He'd clearly underestimated his opponent, and it would be rectified with some old-fashioned surveillance. The diner, located awkwardly on the corner of an alley, he remembered coming to as a child worked perfectly for this mission, as it offered a view of Annata.

The diner was as clearly for the locals as the trendier cafes and restaurants were for the tourists. At least that's what it looked like to Scott when he stepped inside and every head turned to look at him. There wasn't a smile in sight. It amused him a little, but mostly he was bitter. Morello Cove had never been good to him.

Choosing strategically, he went for the booth that had the best view. He ordered a cup of coffee and the kind of greasy burger he wouldn't even know where to find in Los Angeles, and then he started his mission. It was time to find out just how popular the boutique was.

It was popular, he realized a burger, a piece of cherry pie, and three cups of coffee later. Frustratingly popular, in fact. Not only did it have a constant stream of customers, but most of them came out with a cream-colored shopping bag with the name, Annata, swung in lovely cursives on the side. At one point he was even pretty sure he'd recognized one of Hollywood's most famous actresses coming out wearing a large pair of sunglasses and hefting at least three bags.

To sum it up, he was screwed. At least if he didn't come up with a brilliant plan of how to charm, beg and/or convince the stunning Danielle and her as of yet unknown partner that they'd be better off somewhere else, putting all the money The Java Bean Shack were offering them to good use.

Scott liked a challenge, but this had the potential of becoming a headache instead. He wished he'd been more insistent to his boss that he wasn't a realtor, though that argument had only been an attempt to avoid a trip to Morello Cove.

\* \* \*

Danielle kept busy all day. The customers had been a mediocre distraction from her simmering temper, and she couldn't wait to be able to vent to Fleur. Of all the arrogant men she'd ever met…she huffed out a string of Italian swears her grandfather had taught her in a weak moment. To think that this Scott Sullivan thought he could just waltz in and expect her and Fleur to give up everything they'd worked so hard for.

"Did someone rip a dress?"

Danielle spun around, noting with surprise that it was after closing time, which explained Fleur's presence and why she was locking the door. "No, no ripping. Just…" Sighing, she rubbed her forehead. "I need to get out of here. Come over for dinner and I'll tell you all about it. It concerns you every bit as much as it concerns me."

She knew she'd made Fleur curious, but she also know that her friend had enough patience not to ask. Fleur was a saint that way. And she knew Danielle's moods and temper the way only a true friend could, which was a relief right then.

It wasn't until after some fresh air and a glass of chilled white wine that Danielle felt calm enough to explain Scott Sullivan's morning visit. She'd installed Fleur at the breakfast bar with a glass of wine and started preparing a quick pasta dish.

"One of those city slick lawyer types came in this morning just after we'd opened. He was representing a chain of coffee shops and wanted to buy Annata. Buy it!" Danielle slammed the knife down on the chopping board. "As if we haven't worked out asses of to get to where we are. As if it was just some random piece of property. As if...! To hell with him. To hell with him and his dimple and his brown eyes and his...muscles!" She spat out the last word as if it was something revolting.

Fleur sipped her wine. "Well, you told him no, right?"

"Of course I told him no!"

"Then what's the problem? Was he rude? Did he come back to bother you?"

"Well, no." Danielle put a lid on the pasta water with a little bit more force than necessary. "But he just walked in. No, swaggered. He just swaggered in and expected me to hand over the keys."

Fleur's cool look of disbelief made Danielle even more annoyed. "Okay, okay. Maybe he didn't. But he still ruined my day and made me snappy."

"Then I hate him, too. We'll get a vicious watch dog in case he comes back." Fleur slipped down from her stool and went to grab plates and utensils.

Almost all the anger inside Danielle evaporated. She slipped an arm around Fleur and kissed her cheek. "You're the best friend in the world, you know that?"

"I seem to recall you telling me that before, so it must be true."

Danielle finished cooking while Fleur set the table and topped off their wine glasses. When they sat down to eat, Fleur hesitated and sent Danielle a teasing grin. "Muscles and dimples you said?"